2048: A Diary

Works by James Edgar Cherry III

FICTION

Coronado 92

NON-FICTION

Loco For Lizards

SITE

www.jimcherry.com

CONTACT
jim.cherry@gmail.com

Dedicated to Bonnie Jean Anderson-Cherry

2 0 4 8:
A Diary

Being a year in the life
of
Ignatius Fumbo
of
London, England

FIRST SEABYRD PRESS™ EDITION
Copyright 2015 James Edgar Cherry III

Cover Design
Art Direction: Mark London
Cover and interior illustrations by the author

Author's Note

This book contains future slang along with British usages. Please refer to the glossary for definitions.

1 January 2048

Dear Diary,

> *Standing atop a thirty-foot speaker stack in thigh high gumboots and Buckingham guard's cutaway coat, I spied a rabid cyborg slithering from a vent with fire in its eyes, threatening death to all.*
>
> *With 50,000 fans roaring approval of my blistering keytar solo, I held up a hand to stop the band, pointed my instrument at the oily monster, struck an atomic power chord, and shot a pin-thin death ray down its glowing green electric eye. The dying creature's banshee wail harmonized with feedback from my Marshall stack.*

Berrrrrp chirped the phone, waking me from a beautiful dream. I'd fallen asleep with the shade open and Teen Impala on repeat all night. I turned it off, flipped phone to speaker and propped myself up on a pillow.

"It's me." Jelly purred.

"Me who?" I knew.

"Me who has an extra Black Mantas ticket for tonight."

"Sold."

"Sorry for the late notice; I was going with boyo, but we knocked down again. Had my fill."

"Heard that before."

"Mean it this time."

"Cuppa, pre-show?"

"Jammed, can't. Meet you at the station, eight sharp?"

Link Wray's dirty guitar rumbled on random play as I brushed my bent grille in a steamy mirror on the fortieth floor of H-Block Subsidized where I live as a proud Englishman, undaunted.

New Year's resolution: I will collect wise quotes and arrange
them for maximum impact on modern maniacs. Things like
Emerson said:
  Do the thing and you shall have the power.
  They who do not the thing have not the power.
But I can't do the thing tonight, not when I'm seeing Black
Mantas.

The ShowBubble's silvery skin shimmered outside the
soaring arched windows of Marble Cross station. Jelly strutted
across that ancient terrazzo like she's never done one wrong
thing in a brand new leopard-skin pillbox hat and fitted jacket
over a watermelon-suede cat suit that hugged every inch down
to black patent winkle pickers. But even glittering ear buds
wriggling on pearly white lobes couldn't distract from a sadness
blurring Jelly's green eyes that played peek-a-boo through a
copper fringe.

"A-lo Fumbo. Getting it when you can?"

"I'm sorted. You look minky."

"Not feeling it. Cried over boyo all day. Told him, 'Fuck
you, ape."

A fine red rim around her eyes said Jelly was telling it true.
She needed a stimi. We walked into the open-air plaza where
Manta fans in satin and tat sauntered under lead-coloured clouds
scudding through a dead purple sky.

Black shirts loitered in tough guy poses as we paused to buy
stimis from a golden vendi-girl in a bippety-boppety hat. She
looked so good I wished she were real. Jelly waved her embed
to pay and threw off a whiff of jungle night perfume.

"Think she's pretty?" Jelly asked.

"She's a robo. What's in it for me?"

Scowling, Jelly pushed me away, then grabbed my arm and
held fast as we strolled through a glittering arc into the pleasure
dome, like dreamers do. She vibrated with excitement as we
entered the hall under watchful eyes of guards in armored
exoskeletons. Side-hugging me, she said, "So good to see you,
Fumbo. You're more fun than that crepe-head boyo any day."

Every geezer there wanted what I had; I saw it in their eyes.

Surrounded by peacocked peers flashing conspiratorial
smiles, we shuffled in to seats on the second mezzanine. Stimi
buzz came on strong as we sipped while staring at a darkened
stage. *Plastic Icarus* from the Black Mantas album *Two If By
Sea* played hot as we sat in the dark.

A plastic Icarus flew to the sun
On wings that melted one by one
Stimi buzz came on strong as trumpets ballyhooed the Black
Mantas running on stage in glowing, colour-changing suits,
stopping in a v-formation to stroke illuminated, translucent
instruments. An anthem titled *Free Electrons* flowed straight
into *Tsunami Mommy*, a whammy-bar wankathon off their
album *Jagged Little Krill*.

I watched Jelly watch Black Mantas segue into *Sea Hoarse*,
a heavy water chantey Cathode Ray sang to a syrupy slow Bo
Diddley beat. As eerie-sounding cellos sawed their way to a
harpsichord bridge, I wrapped an arm 'round Jelly's bony white
shoulder. She leaned in and shivered like an electric current ran
through her.

Cathode Ray crooned a moody baritone,
Swimming beside you
In deep green and blue
Guitarist Shardz pointed at the ceiling, pulled a rude face,
and wind-milled a power chord that split the ShowBubble roof
in two, scattering a million stars overhead as luminescent space
gas pulsed to the beat.

Cathode Ray crooned:
A sea within a sea
Me in you, you in me
You lay your eggs
Between my legs
"Wot!" Shardz yelped, wind-milling another power chord
while ballistic drummer Kat Man Do thundered through a squall
of electron goo.
An aqua sea
Swallows me
When I drone
I'm not alone
Mezzing on Cathode Ray, Jelly missed a holographic ocean
drowning us in seawater. She came 'round when we morphed
into fish with fins sprouting from our backs and cheek-mounted
gills flapping to Manta beats. Six more songs then lights up for
intermission. We strolled to the lobby under a ceiling showing a
3-D Milky Way. My sponge-soled creepers stuck to the floor
where wobbly geezers had spilt their drinks as I lined up for a
pair of bliterades. "Two Lingering Questions, please." Jelly lit
up like Christmas at the sight of those stimis. We filed in

holding our cups close in a jostling crowd, sat, and sipped while staring at a darkened stage.

Red velvet curtains parted on a watery glass sphere resembling a souvenir snow globe blown up ten feet high. Cathode Ray bobbed inside astride a giant seahorse lit up aqua that changed to purple that changed to ultramarine as he sang Download Ed's swampy title track in a neoprene suit and stylized diver's helmet.

Download Ed
Lived alone in a shed
Deep beneath the sea
Sorting someone's price
That someone was he
Download Ed
Didn't know he was dead

Glimmering creatures of the deep swam amongst the audience as a hypnotic riff looped on. Cathode Ray rose to the top of his bubble, stuck his head out of a hatch and quoted e.e. cummings in an electronically altered voice, "For whatever we lose (like a you or a me) it's always ourselves we find in the sea."

A harness pulled him up sagging limp as a rag doll and swung Cathode Ray 'round 'til he disappeared backstage as the Mantas walked off looking like they were suppressing laughs.

House lights came on and stripped off our fish parts. I stood up on rubber legs. Jelly unfolded her angular frame, stretched her arms up to me and smiled. I grabbed her slender, white, blue-veined hands and pulled her to her feet.

Fifty thousand dreamers shuffled out as one.

"Feel like a cuppa?" I broke the spell.

"Yea, yeah," Jelly smiled.

Ambling deep into the darkened city with our arms about each other's waist, we fell silent. The crowd thinned until we were alone.

"Where should we go?" Jelly likes direction.

"There's a bar I like, the Bang A Gong."

"Yeah. Heard of it. Let's." she nodded.

"What's on with boyo?" I'd waited long enough to sound casual.

"Don't choose so well, it seems. Same mistake, man after man."

"Isn't everybody locked in patterns?"

"Maybe. But how do you crack a pattern? Sick of dum-dum boys, I am. Sick. Sick. Sick."

"Some say love is just neuroses matching up like keys and locks."

"Why not match up good things instead?" Jelly.

"I heard Johnny sells illegals." Always the concerned friend, I am.

"So? I like illegals." She looked at me like I was daft.

"Careful he doesn't rope you in."

"Glad we're friends, Fumbo," she whispered.

We entered the Bang A Gong where a Mystery Girl vid lit the room in soft candy colours. Tightly wrapped in a black vinyl jumpsuit, she clung to a tiny ledge high upside a gloomy looking skyscraper. Her thick orange hair whipped wildly about in a stiff breeze.

"The mask drives our desire," I said.

"No shite, Sherlock. Think she'll ever take it off?"

My favorite girls were together at last.

"Dunno if I'd like that."

"I want to see her." Jelly said.

Zoom to a close-up of Mystery Girl's face in a tight-fitting black satin mask. With her big eyes, petite body, and bobble-head, she looked like an anime come-to-life,.

Mystery Girl wailed,
I walked across a glacier in high heels
Just to feel how the majority feels
But that soon lost its appeal
When I said pull out, he said maybe
Nine months later, we had us a baby
Bad boy and me moved to Portsmouth town
Good town for a kid, but it got us down
Bad Boy sagged like the ungrateful dead
'Til one night I turned and said
Cheer up Bad Boy don't be shady
'Cause Bad Boy, I want your baby

"Wants a bad baby?" I snarked.

"Huh?"

I wanted to tell Jelly about my book, but I ought to write some first. It's lonely at the top.

"The best art erupts when torpor is followed by a mental dam busting through to the other side," I blurted.

"Torpor?" Jelly looked confused.

"A state between sleep and hibernation."

"You think too much."

"What else would you have me do?"

Jelly offered no suggestion.

"Amazing gains in productivity could result from not doing, like a tourniquet effect. Brain yoga. You cut off the blood and pressure builds until you release it and powerful currents flush the sludge, bringing fresh blood circulation to rejuvenate the mind."

"Aren't things different for everybody?"

"Maybe so, but you don't want to be a squirrel, looking for nuts. Finding nuts. Hiding nuts. Looking for more nuts. It just goes on."

"You just go on. Weren't you going to write a book? Why not write about your theory?"

"Nobody wants to be told to stop making their precious artwork."

"That's mumbo jumbo, Senor Obscuro. You just need to put it out instead of stewing in your juices. Sorry if that's harsh."

A lonesome accordion echoed down a mysterious De Chirico street where no one knew my name.

"Anyone can learn to draw and paint or master three chords to bang out a song. I bottle it up until it reaches atomic threshold."

"Rave on, rebel." Jelly looked mildly frightened. "Sounds paralyzing to me."

"By avoiding artistic effort, I'm sacrificing for the greatest good."

"Or are you just copping out?" Jelly asked.

Across the room Mystery Girl belted,

I thought I was smart

I housebroke my heart

Sprouting wings, she jumped from the ledge and flew into an orange sunset as a heartbreak beat faded. So sadly beautiful, it was enough to make you yawn.

"Happiness isn't a destination," Mystery Girl shouted into a roiling burnt orange void as she shrank with distance, "It's an attitude I cop for the trip."

She thoughtfully added, "There are no coincidences," before disappearing entirely.

Jelly said, "I think she's hiding something that's wrong with her face. Fancy her?" I didn't answer. No percentage in that.

We ordered chocolate croissants and sat at a small table sipping creamy cappuccinos served by a self-possessed Asian in platinum pageboy and white leatherette.

"Which do you prefer? Bliss Dogs' a cappella operettas or Death Row Jethro's hillbilly heavy metal symphonies?" I thought she'd have an opinion. She didn't. I tried again, "Which sustains interest over an entire album?"

"I dunno. What's it matter?"

"You have to credit the Dogs for reviving the two-minute single, but Jethro's epics can't be contained in a simple verse/chorus/verse structure."

A cone of silence fell. Her eyes darted away. "Getting late. Work in the morning," Jelly blunted.

As we rose to leave, a Smoking Bones vid booted up. Jelly dropped her purse and went into a sexy sway with her willowy silhouette backlit by blue light from the vid. People stared. When the song ended Jelly grabbed her purse and my arm.

We walked to the tube through soft drops of rain that hung briefly suspended before falling to earth and disappearing forever. I felt her driving, but she was only the wheel.

Jelly turned to me, "Read those lyrics you emailed this morning. Brilliant stuff, but that bit about artistic activity being counter-productive is bollocks." I started to respond, but she said, "Ciao, mister," flashed a juicy-lipped smile, blew a kiss and dropped into a darkened void. She's just suggested I write a book on my theory and now it's bunk?

I stared too long and attracted the focus of a bored black shirt I pretended not to notice. Happy about the long way home, I plugged in ear buds, cued a Johnny Zhivago orchestral and walked a dark, empty street where my footsteps were the loudest sound. Looking puzzled by my smile, a grey-haired Pakistani passed by pulling a spicy-smelling food cart.

Once home I was buzzing, unable to sleep. There was nothing to eat so I checked PeepPals on MemBrain looking for people who might know people I might know. Nothing there.

Pedaled up sufficient charge for a jam, grabbed my trusty keytar and struck koo-koo chords inspired by a night of suppression, Manta beats, and bliterades. Tapping effects pedals, I jammed mountainous riffs over wooded valleys that rolled on to grassy sonic plains 'til I landed on a sandy beach picking a surfside arpeggio that slowly faded to silence. Knackered as a fucked-up pup, I fell asleep instantly.

2 January
Air scrubber's pleading voice woke me, "Please clean my filter. You have thirty-seven hours until system shut down,"

Manta beats pounded in my skull as an air-note floated by: SIT DOWN AND WRITE A BOOK YOU FUCKIN LAYABOUT.

Thanks for the tip, but I can't write hungry. Dodged dinner last night, as there was nothing in the cupboard but a six-pack of Bug-Eata: *Naturally delicious insect protein that'll tickle your taste buds silly*. Dusty pastries baked from the powdered thoraxes of ground-up locusts don't excite me for some reason.

Refrigerator inventory revealed foil crumpled around something I didn't want to see, half a shaker of Parmesan, a nearly empty jar of curry, and a half-liter of Ener-Tea. I looked over at the scanner's half-gone shell and a saliva drip trickle-charged my hunger pangs.

Food good?

Ugh, Tarzan.

Read this sticker on the back of my scanner:
V E G E P L A S T is 100% G.A .S .M:
Genetically Altered Soy Molecules
Not intended for consumption.

It's an open secret you can eat the stuff and many do as it tastes better than bugs. They say you'll go crazy if eat too much, but a little shouldn't hurt. Polished off half the scanner case last week with no problem other than bad breath. I grabbed a screwdriver, detached a panel, snapped off some bite-sized chips, drizzled on balsamic vinegar and added Parmesan for Italian flair.

Eyeballing hovering ad-copters below while munching vinegary vegeplast and sipping tea, their rotating blades told me what to think, but I ignored them, wondering if my book idea would be better as an expose' of the hottest cult going? Any faith that boasts *changing the way you think about religion* has to expect blowback. I should visit the Teletemple and see the steeple; look inside and see the people. No doubt many would like to suss what's going on inside that joint.

Tubed to the Temple, found new members department, got scanned by security and stated my case to an ice queen receptionist in silver jumper, platinum hair, and slanted Scandia wolf blue eyes.

"I'm here to join your faith."

Staring directly into my eyes, she pointed a long, slender, silver-tipped finger down a dark, tubular hallway flickering with vaporous images of television icons John Logie Baird, John Cleese, Benny Hill, Campbell Swinton, David Frost, and some yanks I didn't recognize. Each one softly whispered my name as I passed. Creepy.

At the far end, a distinguished-looking, grey-temple geezer sat behind a glowing, translucent desk smiling with phony cheer. Bathed in soft up-lights tinted a lovely peach tone, his tin god look added to the queasiness, chilling me to the marrow.

Sadly, his phony smile turned into a sincere frown when I leveled about my shaky financials and he sighed a dead breeze that blew down my cardboard dream world. "We believe that, in order to develop spiritually, a Teleternity candidate must first put their earthly house in order. That starts with a reliable income." Of course he's referring to a reliable income they can skim for a reliable tithe.

"Once you establish stability on the earthly plane, you'll have a launching pad to pursue your spiritual development. Until then, I'm afraid we'll have to regretfully decline your application. However, we do appreciate your interest in our faith. Please accept this TeleBible with our compliments."

I raised my wrist omni for the upload and bid him, "Cheers."

"Heavenly beams," he answered; his pitchman's smile beaming brightly through sparkly makeup spackling his pan-dazzle.

Lord luv a duck.

There should be plenty in the Telebible to kick-start my nasty little expose', even without the advantages of membership. On the tube home I cracked open MemBrain to read some of their swill:

Welcome to the truth about mankind's only religion that guarantees scientifically proven eternal life in the heavens. Broadcast technology might be outdated in terms of communication, but it has eternal value as a means of joining in union with the divine.

Non-believers scoff at our rabbit-ears antenna symbol that serves us as the Christians' cross does for them. We hope you'll look past such mockery and approach this TeleBible with the open mind of a sincere seeker.

Realizing that television beams are waves of energy that never decay but sail past earth's atmosphere to travel through space for eternity, our Founder saw this as the solution for man's wish for eternal union with the heavens, a divine inspiration that's become the world's fastest growing religion.

We Teleternists tithe until we accrue sufficient creds to fund Teleascensions broadcast on our GET (God Eternal Television) network.

Please accept our invitation to visit the Teletemple for an introductory lecture and, while you're there, enjoy award-winning stained-glass portraits of television pioneers Philo T. Farnsworth, Alan A. Campbell-Swinton, John Logie Baird, and David Sarnoff alongside beloved saints Benny Hill, David Frost, Lucille Ball, Johnny Carson, Regis Philbin, Heather Locklear and Bud Collier.

A pay-as-you-go religion that name checks David Frost as a major saint? Okay, go. Benny Hill's hilarious, but flying through the cosmos with the corpulent comic for eternity fails to ignite my zeal.

Back at the shack, I checked accounts. Dole was received in time for a much-needed visit to paradise. I triked to Holidaze Bubble where I scanned a luminescent menu. *Your Place in The Sun: a tropical beach sunset guaranteed to soothe a savage bachelor* sounded fervent so I bought a ticket.

I sidled upside a glow bar for a shot of nectar from a gorgeous Polynesian with a nametag that read Eve. She was swathed in filmy translucence that failed to conceal poky breasts I stared at as she poured my ticket to paradise. She handed me an ounce of oily, pineapple/cocoanut nectar that I swallowed in a single gulp. Electric warmth spread from my throat to belly to brain.

I thanked Eve. She smiled and flared my mood ring. I strolled to a locker room and stripped to my boxers. Sons of Martin Denny played as I bare-footed to a fake plastic beach where a pepper-scented ocean breeze blew a sexy mood. I laid down in sim-sun feeling the lip tingle that signals ascent.

The world should always be good like bubbles are, like it was before the troubles.

Surf sounds and gulls' cries jammed a wild symphony as tiny beads of sweat pearled my upper lip and worries evaporated in the warmth of sun.

I didn't care about Jelly, researching Teleternity, nor writing that daft book and had no financial worries, not with my nearness to wicked wahinis swaying to tropical rhythms.

A sexy sister in specs flashed a smile, sat on my lap, repeatedly whispering "Maya" in my ear, she blew away any remaining crumbs of reality. Stopping her wriggling long enough to adjust her specs, she smiled, pointing to a sinking red-ball sun silhouetting a spindly sandpiper darting about on the sand. We melted together as Acker Bilk's *Stranger on the Shore* sound-tracked our kiss.

BLANK! The clock had run out, leaving me in a stark white set of carved Styrofoam and crude vinyl props. Flashing my Omni for another go, Maya smiled as creds were sucked out to circle around and spew a few her way.

We returned to our sweet spot watching stars twinkle in electric-blue twilight above a blackened sea punctuated by phosphorescent flying fish.

Glowing flying fish launched from a wave as a heavenly choir sang *Quiet Village* a cappella. A shooting star crashed to sea, sending up a rainbow cloud that became a giant, slowly turning wheel in the sky with lovely sirens spinning off its spokes. Nothing was as real as ladies that cooed as saltwater dripped into my yap.

I was sitting in a dugout canoe on the shore while gaping at a four-eyed wahini floating down to ease my yearning in slow motion.

Afterwards, Maya rolled off, grabbed my hand and we soared into a deep purple atmosphere where beautiful maidens of cloud stuff gathered around us to coo, "Your head is your only house unless it rains."

"Yes, yes." I nodded.

A ginger-haired pixie in a red plastic miniskirt bedecked with bright flower appliques, a daisy petal headband and bouncy antennae walked me to a beanbag chair and handed me a sweaty steel bottle of ice water. Sprawling knackered, rolling the ice-cold bottle over my sweaty face between sips I felt sweet satisfaction.

You're offered two options for detoxing: go straight in an instant with an antidote at extra cost or sober up slowly for free while watching simulated reality scenes. Retinal scans confirm sobriety so nobody gets out of here high. Either option seemed depressing after the bliss I'd just kissed, but I was skint so I opted for the budget alternative and lolled on a beanbag chair listening to the Stun Sisters' amplified zithers easing my re-entry.

Fellow trippers sprawled about waking from private highs: an over-weight fifty-something geezer in silver jumper and yellow-lens happy specs, an infatuated young couple in matching blue unis, and a worn-out blonde in fake fur miniskirt, gas-charged nails and gel-boots.

A spring meadow glowed through curved floor-to-ceiling walls animated with buzzing bees, swooping birds, and say, isn't that a woodsman in the distance?

Saddened by my reintroduction to reality, I was grateful for distractions.

I pedaled home dodging pods ferrying serious-looking passengers bent on mysterious missions.

With my mood ring spinning purple cosmic love, I felt like a trigger hippie. If Jelly saw me like this, she'd love me 'til Tuesday.

Stopped for a traffic light, I watched protestors trying to enlighten me via street demonstration, chanting:

We are driven by demand
That's our message to the man
We are driven by demand
Street level, that's our scene
We don't party; we are a party
And we're driven by demand
You're the boss
But we're in command
That's our message
To the man

She was pretty so I stopped to listen, "Tensions flare dangerously on the moon. We're raising funds to build the first comedy club there and ease things." Her fierce passion gave her a glow.

"America's breakup left Chinese nuclear missiles targeted on their lunar energy mines. Yank defenses rot because they lack resources to maintain them. There's a squabble over who's to blame, but America's seven new countries just point fingers at each other and nobody does a thing."

Americans struggle to afford the Helium3 they need for atomic fusion and the Chinese grow impatient putting the Yanks further in debt as they desperately scramble to fill energy needs. The yanks suspect the Chinese instigated last year's catastrophic crop failures. Does the King of America have something up his sleeve or is he just spooked by his rival?"

She was a living run-on sentence, pausing just long enough to upload a pamphlet to my wrist-omni. Swore I'd read it and hit delete as soon as she was out of sight.

A moonlight mile later I was home, looking down on a river of tiny moving lights below. Where's everyone going?

A holo-sign shimmered above:

You are kind
You are smart
You love a leader
Who has a heart

I rang Jelly and asked her flat, "What do you fancy in a bloke, anyway?"

"Mighty Handsome Johnny fits my bill. He's the kind that bends a girl over a kitchen table and pleases himself hard while slugging Kentucky Amber straight outta the bottle." Jelly thinks she's funny.

"What's inside a girl?" I asked.

"Sugar and spice." Jelly busted her best dirty laugh.

I programmed MemBrain for Soothing Surf Sounds, put out the light and eased to sleep listening to ocean tides recorded back in the days when they were still our friends.

3 January

I lazed in bed watching an animated presenter run down the Yanks' misery on *CarToon Newz*: As rising sea bites off hunks of America's coastline, they suffer energy rationing, food shortages and stiff inflation on everything but entertainment. History ties us to our former colony, but America's glory days have passed. Now she's a bankrupt family member with endless requests for aid. If they're so broke, why don't they sell Las Vegas off to another country like they did with Miami?

Is bad news easier to take from a puppet? At least it's better than *Clown Time Is Over*, the cartoon weather report.

Hunger tugged me out of bed for a bowl of Nutty Pep Flakes. Surfed for a job and saw that Teleternity is hiring. Sign me up, Satan.

Or, I could work in space. They always need geezers to clean things up. Thank you, World Satellite War for your orbiting scrap heap that inhibits spaceflight, disrupts communications, and rains junk down nonstop.

Got to love those politicos. Like all true artists, they were powerless to resist a fresh canvas. They had to battle in space.

How would you like floating like a dog on a leash while picking up trash, Major Tom? A satellite buster's pay is massive, but you earn every cred. In just a few months I could save enough to spend a year on a beach with a brown-eyed girl, writing a book and sipping rum 'neath swaying palms.

Well-kitted in penguin uni, spats, hard-shell fedora, and scorpion-in-plastic bola tie, I pedaled hot to the Teletemple where I tapped that MemBrain like a samba dancing cock-a-doodle-do, acing their tests. I don't get nervous about exams. I get even.

"The job you applied for has been filled, but we do need a Gleaner of Adversarial Communications. Your psychological profile indicates ease with negative inputs. Job trial's yours, if you want it."

Grinning like a beaver, I jumped to his dimension, "Sir, I'll take it."

The pay is shite, but it's a start. Imagine me inside the Teletemple, getting paid to surf. Collecting slags. Collecting a paycheck. Will it be a made-man makeover or a balmy plot?

The vast army of organized religions, anti-cult groups, concerned families, government investigators, egghead critics, and grumpy clerics arrayed against the Telies should guarantee job security. The tsunami of venom swamping their shores almost makes a geezer feel sympathy.

4 January
Jacked about my new job, I piled on a metallic gray sharkskin uni, tuxedo shirt, tortoise-rim rose-tint monocle, tomato suede Chelsea boots, and granddad's silver watch chain.

I walked a pissy mood to the tube between brooding buildings dotted with broken windows. A drone buzzed overhead, bleeding a trail of holographic homilies. Propaganda whispered from mid-air, walls, and sidewalks — vaporous slogans meant to bully my thoughts. It all piled high enough to make a geezer flip, but I ignored it. I had a job to do.

A busker at the tube entrance wailed in synchronicity.

Woke up this mornin'
Looked around for my shoes
Woke up this mornin'
With the walkin' blues
Thought I had Teleternity blues
But I was mistaken
It was my brand new shoes
That gave me the walkin' blues
Lemme tell you the news
It was the walkin' blues
That changed my views

I got lost in the busker's slide guitar work 'til the Speedliner pulled in and I mashed upside salary men who looked resigned to their fates. Something smelled of rotten fish, but it felt good belonging, even to that lot of stale cods. I took comfort in the fact that I'm not like them; I'm an independent contractor. As long as I can be sacked without justification, I own my soul.

Orientation was eight boring hours of agitprop that felt like someone was drilling a hole in my skull.

Eager to brag on my new gig, I rang Jelly as soon as I got home.

"Which side's up?" I asked.

Jelly sighed, "I woke up feeling frustrated, wondering when's my turn at life? Weaving in and out of traffic like a Formula One ace, laughing all the way, I blew off work and peddled to the QwikCharge where Mighty Handsome Johnny hangs with his dum-dum boys."

Jelly hooks her head up to a machine and thinks on stuff, like I'll be doing. She inspired me to try this line of work.

"Been looking to soap up my opera and it seemed the right time, but Johnny wasn't there. Felt relieved in a way." Jelly seemed proud of her caper.

"Sure to be sacked if you keep missing shifts."

"La, la, la, I don't care."

"Got a new job myself, today."

"Fumbo with a job? What's next, dogs sleeping with cats?"

"You are talking to Teleternity's newest Gleaner of Adversarial Communications."

"You? At the Temple?"

"Yes."

"Dogs really are sleeping with cats."

"Not joining up, just collecting a check."

"Good on ya . . . I guess."

"You might lose your job. Got creds saved?"

"Enough to buy new rags, freshen my hairstyle, and trap that man. Some call him pretty boy. Say he's future rasta. Call him rolling stone. He's just Johnny and he's got a black cat bone."

I dialed volume up on *The Man Who Murdered Love*.

"That song reminds me of monkey boy and I hate it." Jelly pouted.

"Teleternity won't be happy if you can't pay your tithes." I said.

"I'll work it out. *Magic happens when you scan clean*." Jelly quoted her beloved Telebible.

"Embarrassing to die a loser," I replied. "But if that happens to me, blame must be laid at the door of science."

"How so?

"Mum ordered a standard brain upgrade, but something went wonky and bent my brain. Docs discovered the problem early and advised abortion, but she wouldn't hear of it."

"Can't believe you've never mentioned that, but don't worry, you're fine."

Thoughts drifted to Jelly and her target boy. Johnny's the type that ends up in shackles, but even brutal playboys outlive their sentences.

Sipping Ener-Tea and watching smoky inspirational sayings drift lazily to the ceiling: *Tomorrow's your day to win . . . win it all and win it big. Big, I say.*

Random player shifted to Comic Capers. Too lazy to call an audible and stop the madness, I listened.

A rabbi, a priest, and a yogi walk into a bar.

I was sinking fast.

5 January

Home from work, I slipped on pyjamas, cracked a
Guinness, and rang Jelly. "Did you get your job back?"

"As a matter of fact, I did. Slipped into a tiny silver
sheath and marched straight up to the boss while
dabbing at my nose that I'd carefully rouged for full
effect. So sick. You've no idea, sir. Couldn't call, or
even e-mail. I do apologize. Won't happen again,
honestly. I am so sorry!"

"I leaned over his desk doing an Oscar-worthy
imitation of sincere remorse that popped my neckline
open on a lovely lace bra and what lay beneath.
Lowering my head and arching my back, I thrust my bits
out, "Can't I be allowed to be human, just this once?"
while presenting paradise just inches from his reddened
face. I laughed and walked out, exonerated by the power
of breast-nosis."

"Don't make it a habit.' He whimpered as I sashayed
to the door. Think he likes having me around to charge
his batteries. Straight away I was back on the line, dying
for a break and stressing on Johnny, wishing I'd been
sacked after all."

"Solid work, Jel."

"After my shift, I stopped at Johnny's favourite
Qwik-Charge, hoping to run into him accidentally on
purpose. I'd walk up and ask if he'd like a sip of wild
honey. But once again, no Johnny to be found."

"Out bopping and shopping's my guess." It was a
cheap shot, but she's lucky Johnny didn't show. She
doesn't want to know how bad he really is.

"Disappointed, I tubed home where everything's the
same. But I'm going on the hunt tonight."

6 January

Strolling the quay after work, I spied Jelly walking
towards me staring at the ground like she wanted it to
swallow her whole. I stopped and asked her cold, "Are
you blue as you look, Jel?"

"Is it that obvious? I bumped into Mighty Handsome
Johnny at Club Rocktopus last night. Scared him off
when I said sweet things too soon."

"Johnny's the kind that swims free. You know his type. You specialize in his type." She answered with a fake pout.

I asked if she wanted a ride. Jelly whispered "Yea, yeah," jumped on my trike and hugged my café racer jacket. I handed her a pair of ear buds. Pedaling hot, I zipped down Moonlight Mile to a *Get Back* click track. Our best is yet to come and won't it be funny?

My trike's re-gen was working so I put on some speed. We pulled up to the bumper at Milk and Honey Bar where we lounged in a pillowy booth sipping stimis. Newton Minnow Anti-Christ & His Bright Fantastic strummed wah-wah banjos that echoed as if from a deep cave. It was all quite blissful until Jelly heard them take a lyrical swipe at Teleternity. "What's their problem? Teleternity is religion perfected—faith wedded to science. Everyone needs religion, don't they?"

"I just don't see the point of it, myself."

"And why is that?" Jelly's cheeks flushed.

"They insist you live by their rules to score an eternal life, but where's the guarantee? Cut my head off and freeze it, if that's what it takes, but I'd rather find another way." I try not to talk about Jelly's faith, but it's wearing on me because I think they're taking advantage of her.

Jelly rose to the debate, "But Teleternity's different. It scientifically guarantees physical ascension to heaven, and meanwhile, Life-Scans find problem zones so I can perfect things here on earth."

"I don't know what you see in it, really"

"Don't worry 'bout it, baby. I just want to scan clean to be the best me I can be. Then I'll make a video and live forever in space. Don't you want to fly amongst the stars with me?" Jelly's smug smile told me all I needed to know about the wisdom of further argument.

"I'm halfway through their *Entrance* programme. Then I start *Nuance*, and after that it's *Essence*, which is said to be quite unbelievable. I can't wait."

The girl's gone, daddy, gone. Thinking you'll live forever just because your image is broadcast into space? It's a daft notion that I can't channel, but once Jelly's on the topic there's no stopping her. So pretty, she's gotten used to geezers hanging on her every word. Does that make her think she's fascinating?

This caveman must dodge that drone if I'm to preserve my affection. All this I thought as Jelly's rant vibrated at a rapidly increasing oscillation, buzzing like my trike's wheel when I bent its spokes hopping off a curb. Listening to her rant, I fell into a dreamy trance. Then I took her home and listened to her bleat on Mighty Handsome Johnny for another half hour, thinking all the while, *Don't let him take you, Jelly. Don't let him handle you with his hot hands.*

7 January

Woke up shocked to realize that I'm employed. Switched on a chat show, I glued a hole in the crotch of one of my two remaining unis. Second day at work and I've shot my wad clothing-wise.

I've been hibernating, but that's over. Like a freshly-minted butterfly I'll crawl out of a pupa wet and sticky, spread my wings to dry in springtime sun and dazzle predators with flashing colours that warn one and all: I bear poison strong enough to kill.

I washed down a Honey Bug Nutribar with a lemon-berry juice box and headed to the lift.

I peddled through the Teletemple's gates of steel beneath a giant, glowing white rabbit-ear antenna logo. Gotta admire the Telies' Nazis-in-Vegas style, if nothing else.

Walking inside. I felt like a spy on a secret mission. *Don't mind me. I'm just here to suss the service tunnels beneath your tragic kingdom.*

I uploaded health records, pissed in a cup, and watched a freckly-faced nurse stab a vein, passing all tests quite handily.

"Do you enjoy recreational drugs, Mr. Fumbo?" a nurse asked with her delicate 3D holographic fingernail hovering over a translucent MemBrain.

"No ma'am, not my thing, other than a NapTab or two to get some sleep, the odd Stimi to perk me up. Nothing really, unless you count Bubble doses and no one does."

A Human Resources lady marched me in to meet my teammates. "You're part of Tiger Team now, Mr. Fumbos. Time to meet your comrades."

"That's Fumbo actually. It's singular. "

"Sorry. I'm sure you are . . . singular that is." She giggled at her joke. I smiled weakly in my best imitation of team spirit.

"Fumbo, meet Carmen, Joe, and Sue."

Each teammate showed off their workstations in turn, all well stocked with photos of family and self-help slogans. When we came to mine, a name plaque glowed with opalescent hopelessness: I Fumbos, Reaction Gleaner.

Is this all there is to life? To drift along in a meaningless daze of service 'til you flame out and retire? To owe my soul to the company store down to the last drop of properly filtered blood? Such a vacuum-sealed, womb-to-tomb life is unfit for a butterfly that lives but a single day.

I'm being trained to bulk-load anti-Teleternity feedback and structure it into cyber architectures for analysis by analysis teams. Trend lines form blocks that I use to build virtual ziggurat pyramids of gripes from geezers worldwide. Comfortably couched, I ambulate through thought streams of millions that I organize in hierarchies meant for detailed inspections. Virtual reality goggles provide 3D aerial views of info-scapes assembled from atomic bits into molecules that form larger structures. I build blocks from lonely cybernauts' gripes. They pile up into towers tall enough to blot out any sun shining on Tellies' hopes for mainstreaming.

Mighty architectures of repetitive feedback take shape according to frequency of occurrence. Often-occurring key words form keystones. Condemnation of aggressive tithing demands? Pursuing a refund from Telies? De-programming lawsuits? These common gripes provide material for my constructions.

It's draining work as I have to stay on the lookout for stealthy hacker jaguars crawling upside my virtual temples to snatch data, wiping out my efforts. We keep a list of anyone Teleternity considers enemies: journalists, government officials, other religions' goon squads, psychiatrists, and pharmaceutical spies are tracked with laser-like focus by Tele security teams. Things can get ugly.

Cyber surfing through mind fields to build cathedrals of opinion might sound God-like, but their difference engine is breaking down; you can feel it. Recurring funk births bugs that jam the works.

They've got me working on reacts to another currency devaluation, all aboard for fun time. I don't think geezers will stand for it so soon after the last one.

I was in no mood for the trike jam that stopped me cold on the way home, common with so many geezers pedaling about. Some wanker came within an inch of hitting me.

Longing for nothing more than a spot of telly and tea, I broke free of traffic at last and pedaled the last few blocks like a maniac 'til I rolled up to H-Block Subsidized. Happy to be home, I parked the trike and took the lift to my green heaven where I kicked off my shoes and snapped *Floating Naked* onscreen. Ginger beauty Janet Scan-it stars as a nudist who invents a cure for gravity. Every scene a chase scene as Janet bounced about in slow motion, fleeing corporate goons desperate to steal her secret.

She teamed up with a desperate geezer on the run. "Either they own it or they kill it. That's the way of the goon," whispers her partner.

"Maybe so, but them goons never met Janet Scan-it," she sneered in reply.

Her slanted cheekbones, ruby lips, porcelain white skin, and opium eyes revealed no secrets as Janet gulped anti-gravity juice to float about, displaying divine assets in three dimensions.

Floating Naked gave way to *Historic Beauty Pageant 79*, historic lookers re-animated to strut their stuff. I joysticked 'round nature's wild beauties watching Sandy Shores meet Penelope Tree in the shade of a Yum Yum Tree. Damn you, Bachelor Channel. Is this how all hope dies?

Set an early alarm so I'd have time to write pre-work.

8 January

Showered, threw on a robe and pulled a cappuccino. Sipping sweet brown nectar while staring at fluttering air-screen abstractions, I tried to work up a brain to write, but MemBrain's battery sagged. I plugged in just in time for a power cut that shut things down good. Amped on the coffee, I took out a pen and scribbled the start of a manly sex novel:

Wrapping her tightly in his sweaty, sinewy arms tensed with surging lust, Buzz pulled Peaches by her stem, down from a world that didn't care into a funky whirlpool of surrender.

Peaches throbbed with desire as Buzz laid her down on long grass beside a rushing stream. Down, down they plunged, all the way down to love town. They've gotta hard-on for heaven, but they're headed to hell.

Sad, but it was all I had to give. Time to leave for work, anyway. Hopped on my battered scoot and rode hard to where the big wheels turn.

Reclining in a softly webbed chair, I plugged into something that sucked on my brain for eight hours (with breaks). It's better than living on the dole and eating my scanner, if not by much. Still, a month ago I'd have laughed had anyone dared to suggest that I'd be working at the Temple.

The job leaves me knackered and uninterested in anything but diversion and rest. Is this how geezers slide into the big sleep? Cavemen had it better, if you ask me. Their lives might have been nasty, brutal, and short, but they were free of job evaluations, tooth flossing, and air taxes. All our needs are met, but cows have that. Don't bury me now on that lone prairie.

With a sassy new reader-chip sparkling my forehead like a Bombay jewel, I floated through mind-fields of gripes about a religion that so many love to hate, focused today on proposed taxation of religious broadcasts. Seems a bull's-eye shot directly at the Telies. Makes sense, as there's resentment of their insistence on massive tithes for Godcasts. Geezers resent pre-paid rituals that sell ads while maintaining tax-free status.

At lunchtime, the cafeteria offered *Today's Health Plate*. Tried a bite, but couldn't swallow a second spoonful, not even with a quince soda to wash it down. I tossed it in the bin, grabbed a hot nutri and sat there reading headlines off a tabletop screen: *Microbe Eats Human Fat . . . Ultravid Price Cut . . . Robot Brain Size Increase*. The usual. I'm chairman of the bored.

As a freak tide of emotion swept over like an irresistible wave, I laid my head down stifling tears, goosing Quince soda up my beak so I sneezed with hurricane force. Fellow diners turned to stare.

I flushed red when I saw coltish beauty Carmen ankling my way.

"Everything okay, Fumbos?" Her empathy made her seem even more attractive—painfully so, combined with her lush, chestnut coloured hair and dazzling green eyes.

"I'm aces, really. Just a little stressed today."

"Sure of that?"

"Nice of you to ask."

She smiled sweetly, "If you need to talk . . ." and handed me her card.

I was freed at five. In the bliss of release, it struck me that I'm now a regular geezer with a regular job. Wishing to indulge this unfamiliar feeling, I stopped at a Rapido for dinner and joined a long line of fellow working stiffs.

I pedaled home, unable to ignore an irritating hum from bent front spokes that grew louder by the mile. Dear trike: please hold together 'til I log a couple paychecks and get you the attention you deserve. I'll even get your re-gen fixed so you can do the work.

Cosily ensconced in my injection molded machine-for-living forty floors closer to heaven, I switched on Bachelor Channel 3D. Lucky me, *Monkey Dash* was on. Lives there a bachelor who doesn't enjoy watching a bikini girl race a chimp across a giant airbag? After the show, I hit mute and texted Carmen to see if I could suss her scene.

Hi Carmen, this is Fumbo from work.

Who?

Ignatius Fumbo of Tiger Team. I work in the next slot. We spoke today in the cafeteria?

Oh yes, you were crying. How are you?
Better, thanks. Sorry about the waterworks. I
appreciate your kindness today.
Don't mention it. New gigs are stressful, especially a
pressure cooker like ours. Broke down myself the first
night.
How long have you worked there?
Too long, five years.
Doubt I can hang in that long. I'm fried after three
days.
Gets better— it really does. Just gotta hang in. Shock
to your system is all.
Hope you're right. I'll see what shakes.
Felt comfortable, so I took a leap.
Subcutaneous Membrane plays the Zut Club
Saturday. Wanna mob up?
I've something on. Sorry.
Triple NapTabs, eight ounces of purified, and I
nodded out for the night.

9 January
Woke up with a mouth as dry as desert and an axe-
in-my-forehead headache.
Gulped a cup of purified and slipped back to dream
of Jelly and me loving it up behind a bush on a golden
autumn day in Hyde Park. She pulled me off sweetly as
we kissed on the grass.
I showered, zipped on a fresh uni, smacked an Apple
Willpower and took stock:
1. I live in subsidized housing.
2. My trike's a pile.
3. I work for a nutty cult.
4. But I am ready for action, oh yeah.
Pedaling along, I passed the Qwik-Charge where
Mighty Handsome Johnny hangs with his dum dum
boys. Lacking peripheral view with a helmet on, I turned
to see if he was about. Didn't see Johnny, nor did I see
the failure that cut me off 'til it was too late. I clamped
the stoppers. But so did she.
Bystanders gasped at my animal grace as I arced
over the handlebars with Olympic sass. Unfortunately,

my score was ruined when I body-slammed a concrete abutment.

Now I'm trussed up like a meat puppet, sharing a hospital room with three geezers I wouldn't bend an elbow with at the pub watching a sad eco-drama about disappointed turtles in a disappearing sea. I got bored and rang Jelly.

"Fumbo! What color's your mood ring?"

"Speaking to you from a hospital bed."

"What? No! Really? Don't kid."

"A shunt on my trike."

"Sounds horrid. Can I see you?"

Breathes there a girl who can resist a man in traction?

"That would be suitable."

Melancholy turtles swam through my painkiller haze until feeding time when I choked down enough shepherd's pie to satisfy the nurse. As I dug into a lovely blancmange, Jelly showed up looking fresh as a daisy and carrying a fruit basket.

"Which side's up?" I asked.

"Can't get a tumble from Johnny and it's got me blue."

"That monkey's not worth it."

She ignored my comment, picked a bright green apple from the basket, polished it on her plunging-neckline peasant blouse and handed it over, a real Adam and Eve scene.

"Granny Smith, your favourite," she said.

We chatted low volume until Jelly made a graceful exit, leaving me suspended in a string-driven thing and staring at a vid of Mystery Girl swimming through a foggy midnight harbor wailing souped-up delta blues.

I texted Human Resources at TeleTemple and got a robo response, *Your position awaits your safe and healthy return, Mr. Fumbo, but since you haven't yet qualified for PermaCrew, you're not qualified to receive medical benefits.* I'm on National Health so the new pay-what-you-can-plan means creds will be auto-deducted from my salary 'til the hospital's paid off. A single week at work and I'm months behind where I started, financially.

I watched Mystery Girl as pain meds floated my boat gently down the stream. As the meds began to wear off, a travelogue came on: *This is Los Angeles, City of Large Types.*

10 January

Dreamed I was on stage playing a furious Theremin solo with Death Row Jethro. I awoke under mint green sheets in a mint green room with a mint green stomach, still feeling the thunder as Jethro so delicately puts it in his hit, *Peel n' Blunder.* Who could argue with the soulful, jasmine-scented wisdom Jethro wafts our way?

Girl, yer love throbbed code red
When I parked my thunderhead
Inside yer pottin' shed
You bushwhacked this Shadrack
'Til the man took me back
Let's peel and blunder
We'll find our love down under
Where satin and lace
Won't hide our disgrace
Now Jethro's crawlin' down
On hands and knees to exit town
They'll burn this sweaty dog
Like a fireplace log
The band shouts,
Don't bore us, get to the chorus

Double bass drums met feedback shrieks loud enough to crumble pyramids. Haters say all the bombast is meant to cover up Jethro's inability to write a chorus. I say his bombast expresses frustrations better than a chorus ever could. Are we not men?

Nurse Edna rolled up a trolley of fish & chips. I took a plate, munched a few bites, and slipped into a pain-med dream. Came to hearing a doctor and nurse nattering diagnosis at the foot of my bed. The doctor tapped my foot as I came 'round.

"I've discussed it with Nurse Edna. You're quite well enough to finish recovery at home, Mr. Fumbo."

"Great news doctor, but I've got this pain in my ribcage."

"Nurse Edna will give you a scrip."

Wheeled to the lobby for a medi-cab. An Admiralty Pod glided bumpily over pocked streets with an attendant dressed like a landlocked admiral in brass-button uniform with gold brushes on his shoulders and a white skipper's cap. His costume was tattered, but he seemed generally chuffed about life.

When he doffed his cap to scratch his head, he showed off a map of the northern hemisphere tattooed on his clean-shaven dome, while droning on about his collection of butterfly wings. "Ain't seen true beauty 'til you've seen a golden swallowtail under an electron microscope."

Once home, instant-onset bachelor blues darkened my mood ring. I put a kettle on and sat at trusty Casio to bang out a melody. Muse wasn't cooperating, so I took my tea on a thirty-inch terrace of bright plastic grass poking through a build-up of black city grit. *Enjoy the look of lawn with simi-turf*, said the advert that sold me this misery. *Makes any cube's mini-terrace as comfy as a suburban semi-detached's lawn,* they said.

Brightly colored holos dotted the sky advertising Truth-Bombs and Fat-Pads, the usual. A shimmering, vaporous beauty offered soft advice, "Coma-Cocoa is your ticket to a good night's sleep and all its rewards." There's a move afoot to make them stop talking, but I'd miss their sweet chatter.

11 January

Last night I read a book about writing a book that recommended:
1. Make writing a regular habit.
2. Write what you know.

Could my book double as an autobiography if it's thinly disguised and fictionalized? Or should it be a bachelor's companion, complete with saucy jokes, dating tips, and recipes-for-one? Or maybe I should write an expose' of Teleternity?

What's Magic 8-Ball have to say? *Answer uncertain.*

Working a regular job feels like a prison sentence, but maybe I could tunnel my way out by writing a book. I unfurled MemBrain to tap out impressions of

Teleternity, but thoughts danced weightlessly 'til a phone chime saved me. It was my favourite redhead.

"Rang the hospital; they said you were released. Which side's up?"

"All sides are equally trussed up. And you?"

"I'm happy as Larry—got my severance today."

"You were sacked?"

"Played hooky once too often. Girlish charms couldn't save me forever."

"UniCorp's already sacked you. Where will you work now?"

"Knocking them down one by one, but as long as boys think I'm cute, I'll get by. Made some yummy lentil soup. Want company?"

"Hungry as a shark. Soup sounds proper."

"I'll pop over."

Jelly's burned her bridges at both Mega and Uni Corps. What's next when there's just a pair of competing products in each category? By the way, nobody's fooled, wankers. Not really. Would you prefer a Uni micro-cooker or a Mega micro-cooker, madam? A Mega Cola or Uni Cola, sir?

Marketing reflects personal beliefs with the brands of toilet paper we buy. I get the scam, but I'm still powerless against it. My garb is Doom Boy, gear duds by a Uni division that prove I'm a cliché. You won't find Doom Boy duds in a Mega's closet—it's Golf Man casuals, every time. Do they really hypnotize young virgins with their godly chat and well-pressed khakis?

The doorbell rang and I opened the door on Jelly draped in a loose, filmy white uni accented with matte-finished silver jewelry. "Soup's on, Fumbo." She smiled her juicy-lipped, toothy smile, held up a shiny silver thermo, and life snapped into focus.

It made a lovely scene, Jelly sitting beside me with an expression of sweet concern as she poured a bowl of chickpea vegetable soup. A cone of silence fell as we listened to Johnny Zhivago's orchestral croon.

"It's spicy. Mum always made it when we were sick. Said ginger burns out the germs. It makes you sweat and that's good."

Soft light streaming through the porthole lit up
Jelly's face like it shined from within. Used to admiring
glances, she caught me staring and smiled demurely.

My face flushed hot from the ginger soup. Jelly
gazed out the porthole at a holo-ad, so I dialed up
outdoor sound. A giant spokes model purred, "Acme
Home Stomach Pumps on sale . . . lucky is the geezer
who pumps his own at a price like this!"

The holo-lady morphed into a pink cartoon stomach
that contracted and expanded 'til it resembled an over-
inflated football about to explode. Gastric disaster was
averted due to quick application of a stomach pump by
our 3D spokes model.

I started to laugh and winced.

"Have you ever felt like something cool was about to
happen?"

"Enjoying those pain pills are we?" Jelly sighed.

An eerie vibe hung in vague, hospital-smelling air.

She turned to face me with a serious look. My mood
ring spun indigo.

"Fumbo, I'm dating someone."

"So . . . "

"Johnny's the jealous type. I know we're the best of
friends, but he can't handle that."

Rule One: When she starts talking about her
boyfriend, you're dead.

Rule Two: When he forbids her to hang with you,
you're buried.

Jelly stood beside the bed, bearing a serious
expression.

My mood ring spun so violently it heated my finger
and I dropped my spoon with a clatter.

"We won't be able to chum for a bit, but once he
learns to trust me, I'm sure he'll come 'round."

"Not bloody likely."

"Why's that?"

"Any geezer so tight-arsed that he's wedging you off
your chums at the start—it'll only get worse."

A blank mood fell, but I knew how to break the
spell. "Got some pain meds . . ."

"Let's." Has she ever met a drug she didn't like?

"They're on the desk."

Jelly grabbed the pillbot, popped the cap, and swallowed three with water from my bedside tumbler. She put down the glass, grabbed her purse, and smiled. "Rest of the soup's in the fridge. Got an audition for a modeling job. Just might turn up a holo-girl outside your porthole one day."

"Thanks for the soup—and good luck."

"Call if you need anything."

I propped myself up to kiss Jelly's cheek. She swiveled her face so far around that I kissed the back of her head.

Go humans.

12 January

Awoke to a text from Jelly: *Jesus chased the moneychangers out of the temple, after all.*

It's too early for a religious discussion. I texted back.

Your working at the Teletemple bothers me for some reason, maybe because you're not a believer? She punctuated with a smiley.

I tapped out a reply, *History teaches us that geezers love nothing better than building temples, from Babylon to Brixton it's always the same. The architecture changes, that's all. But I gotta get up. Ciao.*

18 January

After spending a week strung up in home traction, I was declared well enough to return to work. And soon enough, there I was, scanning thought-streams, building tower blocks of information and forwarding it all down the line to a chain of fools such as I.

Texted Jelly about meeting for lunch but received no answer. She's probably obeying Johnny's command to stay away.

My explanation of everything might prove more successful with a sexy female narrator, the mysteries of life as revealed by a kitten with a whip. Deep insights couched in popular infotainment, a come-hither bombshell in a .45 caliber black lace bra, shooting soft bulletins of wisdom spiraling into readers' brains, convincing them they've thought of it themselves.

First day back on the job has left me knackered. Tonight will be early to bed, soothed to luxurious sleep by the Simpletones' vibraphones.

Tomorrow I will explain life by compiling bits like this Yiddish proverb: If God lived on earth, people would break his windows.

19 January

Jelly is an expert at self-sabotage. She ran out on her single alcoholic mum at fourteen and lied about her age to strip in a dodgy Soho club. "It was intoxicating, the power I felt dancing. I felt like a star. I'd never experienced anything like it. 'On me lap!' they'd call and I jumped with a smile."

"But sometimes it's a slog being pretty." Jelly continued, "Still, it's the only power I have. Eventually I got anorexic. I'd sit reading recipes off MemBrain, wrapping my imagination round the words, and tasting flavours in my mind. Instead of, you know, actually eating."

Jelly likes to tell me secrets. Sometimes I wish she wouldn't.

"Such a laugh, dancing naked," she said, "customers would promise to 'take me away from all this,' not realizing I made more money than they did. Pulled down more creds my first shift than I'd ever seen in my life. Never felt so beautiful as when I stripped the first time and men broke out in applause."

Should I be shook? I wasn't.

20 January

Jelly rang up. "We are spending the afternoon in Hyde Park today."

"Okay by me, but what about boyo?"

"Sod him. Doesn't have to know everything."

We spent a mellow afternoon watching speakers, walking miles, sitting on the lawn and having a picnic with a bottle of wine before napping under a spreading oak. Later, I won Jelly a stuffed bunny at the shooting gallery.

"Really, Fumbo. I had a blast." She laughed and kissed my cheek goodbye, swinging the pink bunny's arm like a wave goodbye.

I tracked home to a cold *nutribar* and a steaming mug of tea. Still broke. Now that I've got a job the rent is no longer subsidized so I'm working for the cube. Saw online that the mayor's just had his hover yacht's toilet seats gold-plated. Somebody's got to pay for that.

Hungry, but I'm skint. The scanner's half-eaten shell doesn't look appealing.

21 January

Morning sun filtered through a grimy porthole painting my room with buttery cheer as I awoke from a dream of Teletemple goons chasing me.

An air quote floated lazily by:
Someone asked Buddha, Are you a god?
"No," he answered.
Are you a saint?
"No," he repeated.
What are you then?
"I am awake."

I got up, brewed espresso, cracked the Telebible and found this nugget: *Teleternity represents the next step in religious evolution. Its unique combination of self help techniques and guaranteed promise of eternal life leads to fuller lives.*

Meanwhile, It's just a geezer's image flying through space, not his soul, innit? Besides, a frigid black vacuum ain't my idea of heaven. Not to mention that due to ritual Godcasts, the ethers of space will echo for eternity with a lonely grand mum in Kent explaining, *I enjoy knitting Christmas sweaters and raising pet turtles that I name after prime ministers of historical importance.*

Is a person's broadcast image as holy as Buddha's enlightenment? As sacred as Anglican prayer, Hopi chants, and Hindu mantras? Teleternity seems a con royale, but believers are only too happy to tithe away their life savings for beam jobs to space.

Rather save my creds for bubble trips, thanks just the same.

23 January

"Mornin,' saviour." I croaked at a holographic Jesus floating above my bed. He whispered in reply,

They can't get enough of me now
But when I was around
They couldn't wait to mow me down

Jesus looked straight through me for a second before adding, *All I wanted was to love you, baby.*

Time to get up. I'm employed now. Some might view that as a compromise for a true artist like myself. Maybe they're right and I'll slip into a life of quiet desperation, after all.

Situation inventory tells me I have:

1. Funky brain wiring
2. No money
3. No honey
4. Brain-draining gig
5. Worn-out trike with bent fender
6. Pearl white Keytar
7. Practice amp with intermittently working super-reverb

I got manic on a double espresso and tapped out a beat with pencils on a lampshade while dancing to *The Man Who Murdered Love*. Somebody had to put it out of its misery, but did they really have to shoot it fifty-six times?

I took the lift to the ground floor garage, hopped on my trusty *Ultra-Ray* trike, and pedaled downtown to where the big wheels turn. Got to my workstation and reclined supine on an incline to opine on reacts to a religion based on television beams.

Today's blather was meaningless whinging about how our micro-thin membrane universe stacks up like a filo dough of multiple universes un-glimpsed, so who cares about a silly broadcast image? Nerds get lathered up attacking a religion that so many love to hate. Might be tossers, but maybe they're right and we're really just frolicking about on a meaninglessly thin layer stacked up in infinity of worlds.

I drooped, sleepy with boredom. Want a new religion? I say forget those TV beams, try Fumbo's new scheme. What's it all about? I'll think of something, really, just after a little nap. I conked out and woke up wondering where I was. At work! I-am-at-work and I am sleeping. They don't pay us to sleep.

ALERT! SYSTEM OFFLINE! ALERT! flashed my screen. Did I cause this by nodding off? They'll know for certain. They've sacked geezers for less.

Called to a meeting with the shift boss, I walked the hall feeling like a condemned man on his way to the gallows. Entering his cube, I was surprised to see him all smiley with the Divisional supervisor. Do they enjoy this kind of thing?

"Please, take a seat Mr. Fumbo."

The Division-Super stepped over to shake my paw with what seemed like heartfelt gratitude.

"Please allow us to extend the deep gratitude of Teleternity's Online Interests Sector!"

"What?"

"You were so quick to suss that approaching virus. Your fellow workers let it go far enough to eat half our databank. But not you, Mr. Fumbo. Oh no, you logged off and dodged the whole mess, preserving your work and back up copies of your team's entire databank, a brilliant move that saved everything."

Actually, I was dreaming of a ham and cheese sandwich with a kosher dill, German mustard, and a side of chips washed down with a crisp lager and lime, but it seemed unwise to mention that. Apparently all the confusion distracted them so no one had noticed me nodding off. I accepted their accolades with great modesty. This too impressed them. Who doesn't love a reluctant hero? I was awarded a note of commendation, a promotion, and a super-combi-watch complete with scanner, turbo-loader, and five years service. It was all one big strawberry Saturday morning.

26 January
Walking to the tube stop, something caught my eye in the window of an antique shop. *Old But Never Sold* read a hand-lettered sign on a contraption meant for playing those huge "compact" discs of yesteryear. I've collected some for their jacket art, but never had a

player. With my pay raise, I could afford one, so I
stopped in on my way home from work and bought the
machine. The guy threw in some CDs he said were top
hits in their day. Must have been popular to name bands
after food, for I now own CDs by Vanilla Ice, Vanilla
Fudge, Chocolate Watchband, Cake, Strawberry Alarm
Clock, The Seeds, and Moby Grape.

Back in the cube, I plugged in the ancient machine
and popped in disc after disc, listening on headphones.
Okay stuff, but not nearly as good as what I really
wanted to hear, The Inimitable P-Nut Squirrel with their
two girls/two boys/two chords, as God intended. Their
new download, *Why Yes, I Do Feel Perfectly
Understood* climbs the charts like a crazed squirrel itself.

P-Nut Squirrel's electronic Bossa Nova flies me to
Rio's sunny shores where golden beauties flaunt wanton
charms in tropical heat. I dream of Jelly walking the
beach in a wet bikini, welcoming a love injection, "Egg?
This here's sperm. You lot have work to do." Jelly
grows a new curve and Fumbo junior shouts "Lemme
outta here!" before he's even born.

31 January
Tired and lazing about on my day off, I tried but
failed to work up enough energy to fold a pile of
laundry. I was able to conjure just enough juice to study
dust particles floating about in a shaft of sunlight
through my porthole. Dust is everything and nothing.
Those tiny bits could be powdered mummy bones or
ground-up meteor stones for all we know.

I unrolled MemBrain to peck out a lyric.
*Everything turns to dust
Ancient Aztec Temples and lovers' trust
Sailor's curses and ocean's rust
Mother's milk and wedding rings
Ground up dreams and insect wings
Everything turns to dust*
It's all just ashes to ashes, innit? We spring forth
from crumbly bits and strut about for a few score then
fall to earth where we decay back to crumbly bits. They
sweep us up in a pan, toss it in the bin, and that's it,
punter. Magic 8 Ball backs me up on this. But I'm okay

with my decay. *Rage against the dying of the light*, some poet said. What can a poor boy do, but sing in a rock 'n roll band?

Phone chirped, "Hi, it's your favorite redhead. What's on?"

Jelly's voice had an odd lilt. Was she goofing or flirting?

"I was just working up the energy to sort some socks."

"You need to work up energy for that?"

"You don't want to rush into a thing like sock sorting. Want to come my way and talk about it?"

"Now?"

"Early evening?"

"Guess I could . . ."

"I'm down, but what about jealous boyo?"

"We had another row. Sod 'im."

The day sped by as I tidied the cube and compiled a shinky new playlist for Jelly's visit.

"What's new in Fumbotown?" Jelly stepped out of the hall doffing a stylish chapeau with a rotating band lit by captured static. She placed it on the bureau where I watched it dim with its distance from her.

"Big news, Jell—I won second round on SuckerTV. The judges were impressed when I made a radio out of a banana leaf, a scrap of tinfoil and a half-meter of dental floss I found stuck to my flip-flop."

"You're one silly get, ain'tcha?" Jelly trilled her patented dirty laugh.

She refused my offer of cheap champagne, so we visited over tea and biscuits. A not uncomfortable silence was filled by my playlist: Johnny Zhivago's *Mood Swings for Lovers*, Jackie Gleason's *Music to Make You Misty*, and *Digital Folk Hits of the Amazon* in random rotation.

"Life darkens my mood ring, Jel."

"Meaning?" "

"Bored out of my skull at the job. The humdrum's got me bummed. Day-after-day, all I do is shovel data by the container load. We were understaffed to begin with and they've just doubled our workload. This promotion means I have to be responsible and I'm not the type."

1 February
Dreamed I kissed a mermaid in an aqua blue Caribbean Sea. This morning I showered, shaved, and dressed for my role as Salary Man: strange visitor from another world.

Dreams of rock and roll infamy buoyed me as I trudged to the tube for another brain draining day.

Not a technically accomplished player, but his keytar bleats with the heart of a Brixton street lad fighting for his only chance at life. I composed my own review. A geezer needs something to dream on. Hope is a drug and I need to score.

2 February
Left the player on repeat again and awoke to *Elvis in Memphis*. Electric sitar faded as I rolled over in Arsenal pyjamas, greeting the day with a rigid salute from Long John Bullethead.

Especially not feeling the job today. Eyeball-etching lights flood our workstations while air screen refresh rates battle with shutter cycles. Do they scramble our brain synapses as neuro-circuits strain to keep up with conflicting flutter rates? Two nervous breakdowns on our crew this year already. A joke, I'm only kidding. It's been five, actually and one suicide.

6 February
A day off. I woke up feeling like everything Jesus came here to change. Thought a walk might break my funk so I strolled down Baker Street where I saw etched in diamond sidewalk sparkles: *Children are the future.* What's new, pussycat?

All this I recalled, standing in the kitchen as cheesy globs snapped at me from an omelet pan as I folded in tomato and minced onion, and flopped it over tidy as a napkin. Siting down to eat, I logged on a dating site. My profile statement: *I'm twenty-three, broke, and balding. All I need is someone to share it with* has found few takers.

Come sunset, I looked out my smudgy porthole at a massive city teaming with millions of strivers I will never meet. Made me feel like writing: *I threw the monkey wrench for no reason* in letters a thousand feet high.

14 February
St. Valentine's Day? Meant for lovers, not for the likes of me.

28 February
Doing things I'd rather not write about.

7 March
Still doing things I'd rather not write.

14 March
This is my brain on drugs.

20 March - *Down A Rabbit Hole*
A confession, dear diary: like most abusers of illegals, I lied, even to you. Was my brain re-wired under their influence? I don't know, but any excuse will do. We addicts are not uncomfortable with styling the truth, especially to ourselves. Eventually the pain outweighs the pleasure. And then it gets worse. Even knowing that a million sad sacks have trod this same sorry path doesn't help.

Jelly turned me on to something strong and I liked it. Doing illegals with her led to doing them alone. When my needs exceeded her supply, she hooked me up with her boyo and I bought bigger loads from him. All the time, I told myself that illegals are cheaper than bubble trips and you don't have to leave home. It was all quite sunny until it got dark and I became a hermit, never leaving the cube except for work, until I forgot about work. I felt my melon rotting from inside out, birthing strange specters that threw themselves at my cube's walls 'til they stretched like membranes 'round their spooky, stick-like figures. "Can we join yer party?" They'd ask, then say, "Don't be a wanker, and let us in!" I'd turn the telly up to drown them out and watch reruns of *Starring Mr. Stu Bilat* for distraction.

Was my obsession with Jelly driving me mad or was it my broken DNA, or even too much snacking on vegeplast? Could it be a combo, with the drugs thrown in?

All I know is, I was adrift, not practicing keytar, not writing, just watching my rock 'n roll dreams being swept into a dustbin of hopelessness.

25 March / *Haversham's Happiness Nut Farm, Cornwall*

Remember, life is supposed to be fun. If it's not, you've got something wrong. Let us help you make it right, here at Haversham's Happiness Nut Farm

Dear Diary, Sorry about the time gap, but things spun quite out of control. I found it easier to deny the pain I felt wallowing in a drug rut if I didn't write things down.

That tattoo on the back of my neck, *I get high so I can get by* might have been a mistake. Tossing off my uni and running down Camden High Street bellowing plain didn't help much. Authorities frowned. I was sectioned and sent to Haversham's.

Alright, I'm officially barmy, a precipitous drop for a former star employee of the U.K.'s fastest growing religion. Who will love a lad insane?

A matronly admitting nurse set the scene, "Remember Mr. Fumbo, you're not a patient here at Haversham's, you're our guest, just popping in for a little rest, that's all. Soon enough you'll be your old self, ready to regain your rightful place in society."

I didn't mention that I never had a rightful place in society to start.

An attendant showed me to a bunkroom painted in softly contrasting gray and cream horizontal stripes and handed me a small paper cup decorated with similar stripes. It contained three different-coloured pills I washed down with a glass of water. Wrapping myself up in a chemical cocoon is one solution, but obliteration won't be the same without me around. I already miss puttering about the cube and gazing out that smudgy

porthole at Brixton, where I lived as a proud
Englishman, undaunted.

28 March
Afternoon post brought a letter from Jelly, actual ink
on paper. She drew a whimsical cartoon of herself as a
sexy cat on the envelope. Envy blazed in the others'
eyes as I opened it and delicate lemon-verbena scent
wafted across the room. Who sends postal letters to a
nutter? Only my girl Jelly Jam Harrison, that's who.

"You need to accept that Jelly is not the one for you
and accept that your relationship with her is beautiful in
its own way," my counselor said when I mentioned the
letter today.

Situation Inventory tells me I have:
1. Unrequited love for a girl I'll never get
2. An aged trike with a dodgy re-generator
3. An indefinite sentence to a nut farm.

But the jokes get better. Fun fact number one: this
actually is a nut farm. Haversham's is set amidst an epic
English walnut grove. Nuts being a much valued food
source with meat so scarce and suspect.

We work nut farm jobs to defray expenses. I've been
assigned weighing and sealing bags. The packinghouse
serves as hub of circular grounds graced with thousands
of trees planted in precise geometry, Doctor Haversham
testing his theory that parallel lines inspire mental
stability. It's supposed to pacify and help us think
clearly. Windows look out on endless rows of precisely
aligned trees that resemble a textbook perspective
lesson. The walls have contrasting horizontal stripes, as
do blankets, uniforms, even the tablecloths. It does seem
peaceful hereabouts, but that's probably due to the
meds.

They tell us that nuts are proper grub for us
disturbos, nutritional-wise. We're fed nutmeat
sandwiches, prime rib almandine, hazelnut hash, walnut
pie and nut-butter smoothies. Nuts for nutters? It's all
quite sorted.

I like the work. Whistling a happy tune, I watch
others bag nuts I hoist off the belt and place on a scale. I
place the off-weight ones on a second belt for some

other geezer to deal with. Seems they could have automated the entire operation, but left tasks for us to perform as therapy.

We newbies gathered in the auditorium this afternoon. Doctor Haversham took the stage to explain his theory on the calming effect of horizontal lines. The good doctor has a chiseled, hawk-like look and compelling charisma. He projected images of a distant horizon, a sunset over a calm sea, a plowed field at dawn, a whitewashed board house, and a sailboat's lap-strake hull cutting through the water, contrasting these images with jagged graphics, lightning bolts, and rock formations, all to demonstrate that what we see influences how we feel. He said we humans evolved on the savannahs of Africa, gazing at limitless horizons and still take comfort in such. Will this help me grope back to normal life at H Tower Block Subsidized?

After the presentation, I took in a group session. We were told to focus our attention and remain constantly aware of now, and to feel grateful for what we have, however modest it might be. They encouraged us to slow down in order to receive messages from our subconscious. *Do what feels right. Life's a blast / If only you know it* repeated endlessly, along with, *Happiness is not a destination. It's an attitude to cop for your trip.* Are they quoting Mystery Girl? Or was she quoting them? In any case, it's gold for my self-help best-seller that will buy me a new life complete with a stacked-up wife tottering out to the pool in cha-cha heels and a gold lame' bikini to serve champagne. Loving her right there on the deck, I'll plant my demon seed deep in her fertile loins.

1 April
"What is it you really want most from life, Ignatius?" Arlene's expression conveyed sincere concern.

"I was born to boogie."

"Meaning . . .?"

"I want to make music my life."

"Have you worked at that?"

"Not professionally, but I do enjoy playing my keytar."

"Perhaps once you're stabilized we can see about that. What brought you here to Haversham's?"

"I know you won't believe me, but I saw it with my own eyes. One night, while noodling on my keytar, an unholy racket started up inside a wall. I thought it was a neighbor hanging a picture. Then I heard muffled moans. Was somebody hurt? Were neighbours having a go? Moans grew louder and louder until the wall flexed inward like a thin membrane showing outlines of people bouncing off it that stretched like latex around their skinny bodies. They were slamming the walls so hard I worried they'd actually bust into my cube. Though I tried telling myself they're just a side effect of the illegals, they seemed utterly real."

"They weren't real, Mr. Fumbo." Arlene said flatly, but not without a trace of sympathy. "You do realize that, don't you?"

"What was it all about, then?"

"Your tormentors could be seen as symbolic representations of yourself, struggling to break free of psychological walls you're trapped in."

"Anyway, it took awhile, but I finally got rid of them."

"And how did you accomplish that, Mr. Fumbo?"

"Couldn't believe it worked, especially after all that I'd tried: blasting music loud enough to crack plaster, swinging a smoking sage bundle 'round the cube 'til it set off a smoke alarm, chanting in a language of crystal blue persuasion, and drinking herbal teas that tasted like retch. Finally, I tried whispering. People really listen when you whisper. Even the wallys paid attention when I got all low-volume and conspiratorial. They hung on every feathery confidence as I sucked them into circular logic leading to the fact that they simply had to go and soon. Somehow it worked and they left."

"Interesting." Arlene leaned in, looking at me like I was a bug.

"Are wallys the price I pay for having an imagination?"

"No, Mr. Fumbo. Imagination is a wonderful thing. Without it, we we'd still be digging in the dirt for roots to eat, wouldn't we?"

I fell silent.

"What brought you here to the Farm, Mr. Fumbo?" Arlene leaned in close, raising her eyebrows in an encouraging expression.

"Every night I'd tube home from work, dose myself with illegals, then conk out with the telly blaring. Got so knackered I started buzz-bombing devil's tails for a pre-work charge of energy. It worked miracles—I was massively productive for a while. Then it turned on me and became destructive, affecting my work. A showdown came down when I nodded off a second time during a shift. A sneeze woke me up, my arm spazzed and hit DELETE at the worst moment. A warning prompt came on, " DO YOU WISH TO DELETE? THIS ACTION CAN NOT BE RESCINDED!" I sneezed again, spazzed again, and hit the button a second time—just to make sure, I guess. 'Christ, no! Do not delete!' I yelled.

They sent me home for two weeks' suspension without pay.

Of course I was different than others who got hooked. Drugs couldn't fasten their grip on me. I just needed a little something to wake up for work, and maybe a little something else to power my writing when I got home. Writing had bogged to a standstill 'til I started doing illegals. Creating a book seemed to be my only ticket out of zombie life at the Teletemple. Didn't Kerouac do drugs? De Quincy, Capote, Burroughs, and Bowie?

Smoking devil's tails, I cranked out a fat chapter in a week. But hyped like that, I couldn't grab a kip to save my life so I took innerludes to help me nod. Of course, innerludes dictated the purchase of a ViewBrolly, one of those home bubbles you unfurl over your bed. Came with a three-pack of programmes: *Tahitian Temptation, Skye Dive*, and *Route Sexty-Sex*.

Sitting on the edge of my bunk, breaking caps under my nose to breathe sweet vapors, I laid back to trip through sultry scenes populated with sexy love things—

like a bubble trip at half the cost. Not to mention the luxury of doing it at home.

Innerludes left me foggy in the morning, so I doubled my dose of devil's tails in order to wake up proper. It was a circular route to hell."

Arlene stopped scribbling and looked up, "Thank you for your candor, Mr. Fumbo. You've certainly given me plenty to work with."

"I just needed a little something."

"Of course you did."

2 April

Things are cosy here at the farm, even if I feel like a raisin in the sun. Will I soak up ultraviolet 'til I desiccate entirely and they sweep my leathery scraps into pile where they plant a sign; *Here lies Fumbo, dry as his dreams*? An ocean breeze will blow away a sad pile of elements that once walked like a man. Swept out on the tide, I'll mingle with the dark and briny 'til I'm breathed in through the gills of a hungry shark diving for frightened tuna. Breaking down even smaller, I'll be absorbed by phosphorescent plankton and swept up in a glittering arc by the arm of a beautiful native girl swimming naked in moonlight off a beach in the Yucatan. That is, if seagulls don't gobble me up and poop my digested remains onto the windscreen of a Nissan Cilantro first.

4 April

This little respite might be a perfect setting to finish my book and publish it when I'm released. The world will quiver in awe before a man who laid it down to stay. No longer will I be a mere wanker on the dole; I'll be a literary star gazing down from on high, shooting out love beams to Arab and Eskimo, Scot and Jew: Love to all God's children from a man who knows their joys and pains.

I borrowed a MemBrain from the library and emailed the chapter I'd written during my drug daze to five publishers. One replied today. Believe in miracles, you sexy thing.

Dear Mr. Fumbo,
Thank you for your recent submission.
We so admire your parody philosophy chapter and,
interestingly enough, currently seek a writer in that
style. Based on the obvious flair for satire you
demonstrate, we have an assignment to discuss with
you.
Sincerely,
Ms. Ann Caruthers
Vice-President, Acquisitions

Haversham's Happiness Nut Farm Media Centre set
me up a vid chat with Ms. Caruthers, a roly-poly aunty
type in a flouncy, high-collared satin blouse and
bejeweled eyeglasses that glittered beneath a nimbus
cloud of steel-grey hair. I thought she was spoofing
about my "philosophy," her company is MemBrain's
number one publisher of joke books for the loo. But
looking in her one good eye (moving roughly in synch
with the real one, a flesh-coloured patch with an
animated hologram of a matching eye covered her right
socket), it was plain that Miss Caruthers meant every
word. "In fact," she added, "feel free to spread bits of
your deep thoughts about to break things up, like
potatoes in a stew."

I couldn't fake a laugh. At least I'll be readable on
MemBrains everywhere. Disregarding vague feelings of
humiliation, I smiled agreement with my would-be
publisher.

Seeing my book climb a list of top downloads is just
what I need. So what if it's not a ponderous philosophy,
but a gag book for defecators?

"Titled 'Way More Laffs for the Loo Than Anyone
Thought Possible, Volume Seven,'" yours will be the
latest title in our current series and the forty-ninth in our
distinguished Laffs for the Loo series overall." Miss
Caruthers puffed up, "We've published so very many
successful series, Laffs for the Loo, More Laffs for the
Loo, Even More Laffs for the Loo and Could There be
Even More Laffs for the Loo? But if you ask me,
Another Book You Wouldn't Read Unless You Were
Otherwise Occupied would be more accurate." She
chuckled a gurgling laugh that sounded like she was

choking on a haddock bone, a chortle that carried on so long I thought she might need a Heimlich.

"If you don't mind me asking, what happened to your last writer?"

"Oh, she got all huffy. Started demanding royalties, 'Not writing anymore shite books until I get a bigger share of the shite pile,' she said. Can you imagine?" Ms. Caruthers chortled again. "So we flushed her and went looking for a replacement." She laughed even louder this time. "Now, unless you're the greedy type, you'll find that you can make up in volume for our modest individual book fees."

Miss Caruthers chuckled again as a goodbye.

Getting published on a big site like hers will be big shite indeed.

7 April

B. K. Bledsoe, Stumpy Timbers, Bedford Vann and I sat like monkeys in a row awaiting entry to the Activity Center, or as it was called for this special night, *Midnight at the Casbah.*

Though he'd sold us a plan to get extra loaded on pills that we'd saved from daily doses so we'd be cool and impress the ladies, Nicotine Nic was strangely absent.

We sat waiting for a chance to dart to a corner of the loo away from security cams, retrieve extra meds we'd randomly swapped, super-sterilized, and swallow with glee.

It was the afternoon of The Spring Fling, an annual dance with the lovelies of the fem wing—said to be the most exciting day of the year here.

The Spring Fling is our annual, one and only chance to get acquainted with the ladies next door. The rest of the year, authorities strictly enforce a ban on coed mingling so we only catch fleeting glimpses of the delicate disturbos through a wire fence between our exercise yards. Mates and I planned to double dose and swap meds with each other in order to present our most confident and witty selves, thus showing the ladies what suave gents we are behind our usual blank stares, random drools, and shuffling gaits.

Unfortunately, Nic's plan proved flawed when the meds we'd hidden in our nether regions dissolved into our tender bits, blitzing us prematurely from the arses up. We got so loaded that all we could do was drool and stare with droopy-eyes as our objects of affection filed past us into the activity hall.

"Angels fallen to earth . . . " Bankrupt Bledsoe slurred before collapsing onto his side for a snore.

Just then, Nicotine Nic rolled up disguised in an Elvis mask and gripping an electric bullhorn so hard his knuckles went white. He drew the plastic cone to his lips, pulled its trigger and, overly enunciating in a loud-enough-to-shatter-windows, electronic tone said, "Nicotine Nic at yer service, ladies. Prepare yer lovely loins to fit me pipe. And fear not, me love knob bears sufficient joy juice for one and all. All right, roll up now. Lucky's the girl who's first!"

Did Nic's bold assertion of sexual prowess represent a deep insecurity on his part, or just a case of bad judgment? The lads muttered astonishment and the ladies' reaction was even harsher.

Though we're all certified nutters, we were nonetheless impressed by the deep barminess Nic displayed. And he wasn't done yet. Keeping the bullhorn pressed tightly to his lips, he launched into a tune he'd obviously spent some time in crafting:

I'm your pie-eyed pleasure guy
I'm Nicotine Nic, am I
And I've got charms you can't deny
Packed up sweaty in me briefs
You'll find the tool for ladies' relief
So ladies, won't you listen
To a man with a perfect piston?
I'm Nicotine Nic and I'm a perfect fit
And just like fags, I'm hard to quit

Nic started slurring halfway through his song. Before reaching the chorus, he keeled over, made wet smacking sounds, and launched a roaring snore amplified loudly enough to rattle windows.

We sat still, silent as Easter Island statues. Somewhere off in the distance, a dog barked.

This was such an uncharacteristic outburst from Nic that I began to wonder if it really was our beloved chain smoker under that mask. I crawled over and ripped his latex off. It was Nic all right, sawing logs as contentedly as a newborn babe. Unfortunately, he awoke enraged at my action, jumped me and, straddling my torso with his little legs, pummeled my face with his tiny, tobacco-stained fists of fury. I reached for his neck but he slipped my grip. Finally, I bucked him off like a rodeo cowboy, pinned the pint-sized puffer to the ground, and counted off a win.

White coats arrived and pulled me off just as I finished my count. Nic had given me a black eye and a swollen nose. After he was hauled off to detox, the rest of us were herded into lockdown. The ladies watched the whole thing with their faces frozen stiff in horror. B.K. Bledsoe spoke for us all by shouting to them, "Poor dears, you'll never know what you've missed."

"Next year, mates," murmured Bedford Vann.

A young nurse wearing black plastic NHS specs swabbed blood from my nose and jabbed me with a needle full of happiness.

10 April
Woke up feeling wound up tight as linguine around a spoon. Been feeling fucked up since the multiple drug abuse of my night at the Casbah.

Had a session with my counselor and told her, "Though it seemed a good idea to work at the Teletemple, things soon turned bad. Did job stress cause my crack up? Or was it head damage from the crash? Something made me feel reluctant to leave the cube until I gave up everything but work and illegals. Then I gave up work.

For a while there, it seemed like quite the sparkly lifestyle. Anyway, I had a book to write and pep drugs could help. My first week off, I stayed high on devil's tails, pounding MemBrain's keys hard. I was on fire, forcing out a single diamond-tough chapter. If the wallys hadn't shown up to bedevil me, I might have finished a whole book."

Jotting furiously, she didn't say a word.

It was daft to think I could use this as a writer's retreat. Who writes deep philosophy doped up on meds? Got that shitters' book to write anyway, ought to be able to squeeze that one out.

Watching *News of the World* on a cafeteria telly, I caught a very bad flash indeed; Florida authorities have announced that heavy mental rock star Death Row Jethro was found dead by the banks of his own lagoon in the Everglades. The popular singer left a suicide note stating, "I hate my job." An autopsy has determined that Mister Jethro expired due to an overdose of shotgun pellets in his brain. His pet alligator Brutus was found still leashed to his wrist in good shape. Brutus was sent to the Sarasota Zoo where he's reportedly doing fine.

"He's reportedly doing fine." That's nice, but it breaks my stride that Death Row Jethro has earned his name at last. I retired to my bunk, grabbed a pen, and penned a poem to a geezer we'll never see the likes of again.

He wanted to bore a hole in the planet
So cool and dark they'd ban it
Bore through oaken verdure and bedrock granite
He'd blow clean through to China one day
Show the Buddha man a blinding ray
He wanted gold, leather, and blonde
A room with a view and a house with a pond
He knew he could top Elvis, if only we'd listen
So he bored a cylinder to fit his piston
But when it was all over
When it was down to sink or swim
Jethro didn't wear the coat
The coat wore him

12 April
Will guest Ignatius Fumbo please report to the visiting room immediately? You have a visitor.

A squawk box commanded me to get out of bed. It had to be Jelly. Who else would call?

Pine-scented fumes from a cleaning crew stung my beak as an orderly wheeled me down a long striped linoleum hallway to the visiting room. A gorgeous, exotic-looking bird wearing a tiny, feathered hat perched at a saucy angle sat bolt upright, primly cleaning her specs. She looked up as I rolled up.

"Hello, Mr. Fumbo, I'm Lilly O'Lilly of Teleternity Cares, our mental health outreach and I've been assigned your case." I watched her silvery hat feather wave along with perky movements of her head like it was interpreting her words.

"Pleased to meetcha." I extended a paw. Smiling with cherry-red lips framing her pearly whites, Miss Lilly shook it with a delicate bird-boned hand.

"Teleternity Cares helps employees who find themselves in difficult straights work their way back to normal lives." Dividing my attention between her sexy mouth and that bouncing feather, I only half-listened to Miss Lilly.

"Do you understand, Mr. Fumbo?"

"Oh, yes. Yes of course, I understand, very much so. You can help me, Miss Lilly?"

Miss Lilly paused dramatically, locking her azure pools on my watery grey eyes as if gauging my sincerity.

"So, you can spring me outta here, then?"

As I waited for her answer, Miss Lilly stared at her fingernails, analyzing each one minutely before filing it with surgical precision. She spoke without looking up, "Well, that's rather more in your hands than mine, but I do stand ready to help. Would you like me to help you, Mr. Fumbo?"

Miss Lilly finished her nails, held her hand out for inspection, stuffed the file in her purse and leaned forward to determine my receptivity to her offer. I couldn't tell if she was scheming or sincere, but I've nothing to lose by going along with her.

"Of course. I'm ready for any way to get out of here and back to life."

"That's super, just super, Mr. Fumbo. I'll sign you up for our *Course in Confidence*, a therapeutic instructional that I just know you'll find most helpful. You can source it in the MemBrain Library."

"I'll do my best." I bleated gravely.

"Yes, Mr. Fumbo, I do believe you will do your best. And I also believe you'll prove releasable in due time, given your dedication to our programme." Miss Lilly punctuated her upbeat ending with a broad smile.

Releasable. Have to like the sound of that. She said they could do so because I never got violent. Pressure just kept building upside my melon 'til my hat didn't fit and they dragged me here to swallow pills and bag nuts.

"There's just one thing . . ." Miss Lilly leaned forward again as if to add special emphasis.

I leaned in eagerly, "And that would be?"

"I understand you've been offered an opportunity to write a book?"

"No threat to Dickens, but I'll be published and that means a lot."

"Your ambition is a healthy sign, Mr. Fumbo, but I've consulted with the staff. We will encourage you to take up professional work in due time. We just don't feel you're quite ready for such pressure at present."

"Meaning?"

"As your appointed care givers, the staff has informed Miss Caruthers that they will contact her when they feel you're well enough to take on professional work."

I was so close to immortality, Dear Diary, but my caregivers don't think I can handle writing a joke book for shitters? We will encourage you to take up professional work in due time. Sod the lot of 'em. I see their limits now. Back at my bunk, I swallowed an extra dose of happiness I'd tucked in a hollow of the bed frame.

Soon the meds kicked in like a big bass drum and I was buzzing good like an inpatient should, listening to the Sounds That Rebound channel. Dear Mr. Fantasy, s'cuse me, while I kiss the sky. I'm 2000 light years from home and the beauty of time is that it's snowing. Koo-koo-ka-choo. Koo-koo-ka-choo.

Who needs to write a book? I'm happy as Larry hanging with my nutty buddies here at Haversham's. I can wait the witchdoctors out if Miss Caruthers can.

The measure of a man is, can he write with a hangover?
~ Ernest Hemingway

I say the measure of a man is: can he write while surrounded by raving nutters and pilled to the gills?

Nothing expresses mystery like poetry. My book, "Mount Your Own Wheel and Ride It Because Life Is a Journey, After All" might work better as poetry. Humans have consciousness so the universe can look at itself through our eyes. What rhymes with that?

Bedford Vann's a quiet man, but we've nonetheless become chummy since our jam—at least as chummy as you can get with a geezer who spends most of his time sulking and sleeping. "Rhythm gives you a way to swing through life. A man loses his rhythm, he's lost everything," he shared some wisdom at lunch today.

Miss Lilly O' Lilly described my challenge here at the farm as "making lemon tarts from lemon parts." Okay, but writing that loo joke book would have made a good start. That won't be happening with these busybodies riding my ass all the way down to zombie town. Is that where they want us to stay?

Picasso said art grows stronger with resistance. If that's true, maybe it's good that they forbid me to write in here. I'll gain massive pent up energy and pound that keyboard with atomic fury once I'm sprung.

14 April

Sitting with Bedford Vann at lunch, I felt like making some noise, so I asked, "Fancy a jam after vittles?" Could have guessed his answer.

"Not bloody likely." Mister Gravitas laid it down to stay.

"Not feeling musical, then?" I was hoping he'd have a go.

"Done with music, mate. Dead and buried."

"Too bad. That was a blast the other day."

Bedford grunted something that sounded mildly positive and returned to slurping his split-pea-with-ham.

I'm adrift in a blue canoe with nothin' to do. Got a load on my noodle and hair like a poodle. Making music could be therapy. We could have got something on, Beddy pounding a hatbox while I be-bopped beatnik jive and stabbed at a keyboard.

Bankrupt Bledsoe looked alarmed at our conversation. After Beddy left, he whispered in my ear, "Watch that man. He could eat you with a fork and spoon."

Stopped by the mailroom and picked up a note from Jelly, then padded to the sunroom in floppy canvas National Health slippers. I carefully prised open the lavender envelope so as not to tear its delicate, sandalwood-scented paper. Geezers stared, but I froze 'em frosty 'til they turned back to watching springtime swifts dart amongst swaying branches.

Jelly didn't say much, but touched that she wrote, I carefully folded her note and placed it back in its envelope, closed my eyes and soaked up balmy sunrays beaming through a skylight, thinking on her and old times in London. Thought I was miserable then, but it seems a paradise from here. I fell asleep and dreamed of a summer day rolling with her on long grass as distant jungle drums pounded hot rhythms.

Awoke up to drumbeats from the activity room. That could only mean one thing. I rushed over to stand in the doorway and watch Bedford Vann punish a box top with a pair of pencils, pounding rhythms divine, humming as if in a trance. Our whole lot mobbed up to dig his scene. Eventually Beddy looked up, saw us watching and dropped his pencils, but not before flipping one in the air, catching it in his teeth and smiling brilliantly. Bedford smiling? A chill ran up my spine. We all clapped. Bedford wiped his smile off straightaway but old stone face had cracked and he couldn't take it back. We'd caught him out at last.

Here at Haversham's, our days blend one into the next in a blurry chain of medicated isolation. With patients doped up like this, wild things go down. Minor issues grow major and major ones blow up burly enough to blot out the sun. I try to steer clear of drama and keep an even keel. Watching telly, weekly papier-mâché' classes, *Fun With MemBrain Hour*, and nightly vids are my only islands of relief on this twilight cruise.

15 April

A strange new patient arrived today. Standing before us with a shaft of sunlight illuminating his ginger Afro like his head was on fire, he cleared his throat, "I am Sparky Fuego, your plasticine purveyor of playfulness, your peppy Pollyanna and self-appointed joy-buzzer supreme, a ginger cyclone in kilt and tam at your service, twenty four-seven. I'm here to write the songs that make the whole world sing, so to speak."

"So, you are Mr. Ignatius Fumbo, eh? So very glad to make yer acquaintance, sir." Sparky stood close enough to spray spittle on my cheeks while squeezing my mitt so hard I felt bones I never knew.

"Have I mentioned me blood type and motto are one and the same? 'B' positive!" When I looked puzzled, he added, "Get it before it's gone," and his booming laugh filled the room.

I rubbed my bruised paw. Sparky looked straight in my eyes, softly whispering "Sinceeeeeeere," as if it was his last breath. He went on to repeat this routine with each and every patient in our wing 'til my stomach turned with the serial insincerity of it all.

"So, scouts, who will lead our little song today?" Our porky Mr. Congeniality croaked an unwelcome invitation through his yellowed grille as we assembled for lunch. Can't he see that we live only for pills, telly, and the odd blancmange?

Sparky has appointed himself our resident cheerleader, but his act's not going down well. His attempt to lead us in a chorus of Every Dog Has Its Day fell quite flat. If this were a movie I'd cue a Theremin swoon to score the eternity that passed as Sparky's exhortations were met with the quiet of standing stones. We stared at the floor until, blushing red as his 'fro, he joined in our inspection of the parquet. Soon enough, he'll be a shuffling zombie like the rest of us and that can't happen soon enough for me. But to give Sparky credit, the universal distaste we feel towards him bonds us closer than ever. He presses on regardless, refusing to slow his charm offensive for an instant.

"I propose a toast to Juan Garcia Esquivel, book-ended with Spike Jones as the greatest musical pioneers of the 20th Century." Sparky proposed a juice-box toast during lunch. No one cared enough to respond.

"He's a puddle of chub with a head on top." grumped Stumpy.

"The new man's a plant," Nicotine Nic stammered, "sent here to drive us all crazy."

"But we're already crazy," B.K. Bledsoe countered.

Stumpy Timbers confided that he was plotting to bring the braying Mr. Sunshine down, but suffered a creative block and the moment passed, "I'll think of something in the morning," he offered as an excuse.

"What's on with the ginger?" Bedford muttered as we crawled into our bunks at lights out. Stumpy Timbers, whose bunk lays directly over Sparky's, leaned over the edge to express himself more directly to Fuego, "We were doing just fine without you here, Tubby. Do us all a favour and stuff it, okay?"

16 April

After lunch Sparky popped out a pair of bongos and sat beside Beddy at the craft table. "How's about lesson, mate?"

Bedford grabbed the drums and pounded a rhythm tight enough to bend time and space as we all gathered 'round to watch. He finished with a flourish. We clapped heartily, but nobody said a word. Beddy stared at the floor, but I could see that he was smiling again.

17 April

"Craving a cappuccino, mate. How about you?" Sparky asked after breakfast.

"Nothing would suit me better, but coffee's forbidden." This prohibition proved but a minor inconvenience to Mr. Fuego. Two hours later, he was crouching under the craft table twisting the handles of a shiny sliver machine and pulling us cups of sweet black espresso suitably capped with proper crema, milk and foam. I stirred in a lump of raw sugar and sipped a heavenly brown nectar with great relish.

After pulling everyone coffees, Sparky handed out pens and paper, "Thirty minutes to write down thoughts, poems, stories, do a drawing, whatever you like. Then

we'll share, one after the other." Most favoured
Sparky's idea, but Bedford Vann headed off to the
sunroom and Bankrupt Bledsoe waddled off saying he'd
rather watch cricket. As for the rest, Nicotine Nic
expressed our mood, "Good for a larf." We were so
happy to have coffee, we'd have agreed to anything.

Our recitations went down a storm, each and every
one except for Stumpy Timbers who repeated his excuse
about meds dulling his creative powers and told stale
jokes instead. Everyone gave as good as they got and
laughed up a storm.

"Does his own stunts, that Sparky," summed up
Nicotine Nic.

19 April
Things started out innocently enough last night when
Sparky Fuego turned up a Chinese checkers game. Once
again, amazing us all as competitive games are strictly
forbidden, especially ones with dangerous bits like
marbles.

We decided to stage a tournament. Halfway through
the first game Nicotine Nic accused Stumpy Timbers of
cheating and started up a row. Everyone chose sides.
Marbles flew at lethal velocities. Someone scored a
freak shot straight down the throat of poor Nic just as
Nurse "Boom Boom" Bellwether rounded the corner to
check on the racket. Seeing Nic gasping for air, she
squashed her fulsome bosom firmly upside his scrawny
spine and Heimliched the holy shite out of him. He
grunted a manly grunt and shot the marble out of his yap
with enough force to shatter a nearby window. Nurse
Bellwether screamed like she'd been shot herself and
laid on the drama, pressing the back of her hand to her
forehead and rolling her eyes. When she released her
grip, Nic slumped to the floor like a sack of potatoes.

"Good on you, Nic," Stumpy extended his hand to
help Nic up.

After things quieted down, I noticed Bedford Vann
staring at his hands, turning them over this way and that
like he'd never seen them before. He picked up a pair of
wooden pencils and walked to where Stumpy sat
dabbing his bloody nose.

Beddy started beating out a fierce rhythm on Stumpy's protective-therapy helmet. Stumpy joined in by opening and shutting his mouth to vary the acoustics of his hollow head.

I threw down some freestyle.

Sparky Fuego means it, man
He blew out the Nut Farm checker ban
He says snow when it's rain
And pleasure when it's pain
And he really means it, man

The others gathered around to dig our act. They clapped when Bedford nodded a signal and we stopped dead on the beat. It was cool like jazz.

No one speaks of it, but I think everyone has suspicions of who Bedford Vann is, or was. What luck to be sharing a bunkroom with him here.

After dinner, Sparky Fuego asked me about Bedford, so I filled him in, "The Black Mantas were Bedford's invention, but as they began to taste success the keyboardist and singer formed a power block and froze him out. While packing for a flight to record their first album, they forced him from the band. A press release cited the usual musical differences before adding, *Bedford Vann plans to pursue independent projects.* Being their chief songwriter, Bedford held a power position the keyboardist and singer wanted for themselves. They claimed he lacked the proper image, but that's daft. He's got a great look with his Afro-Caribbean black skin, smashed-in beak and suede melon."

"The Mantas sound like absolute rotters," Sparky shook his head, "tough luck for Bedford."

"Yes, a very bad break indeed. Black Mantas hired a drummer with a teen-idol look and went balls-out for the pop market. How shitty it must have been for Beddy, being sacked just before his band broke big after years of shivering in the back of vans as they played every piss hole from Birmingham to Brighton."

"Reckon you can't blame him for losing the plot." This all came as news to Sparky.

"Black Mantas flew off to the Bahamas and laid down the triple titanium *Download Ed* album based on

Bedford's brilliant songs, but he wasn't there to bask in the glory. Music sites delighted in chronicling his headfirst dive into a vat of illegals, never resurfacing 'til he'd lost the plot entirely. Didn't help his case when he dressed as a clown and ran into a tube stop to spray BLACK MANTAS ARE ROTTEN FISH down the side of a tube car. In and out of rehab ever since, he must be living off royalties from his songs on that first album. But all the creds in the world aren't much use to a geezer stuck here in Haversham's with the zombie blues again."

22 April

Sparky Fuego's charm offensive is bringing the lads 'round one by one. Even perma-frosted Bedford Vann has warmed up to the point that he's regularly grooving with the bongos Sparky smuggled in.

Sparky showed us how to hide pills under our tongues and pretend to swallow them while orderlies watched. Since we've been dutiful little zombies up 'til now, they've grown slack in checking. After the attendants leave, we cough the pills into our hands and flush them down the loo where they belong. Fortunately, authorities never sussed the true depths of Sparky's subversion, but they did discover enough to scare them. They didn't like his effect on us—seemed almost jealous of it. By subverting their control, Sparky provided them with the perfect justification for what they did. Smuggling in coffee, popcorn, beer, Chinese checkers, comedy vids, football replays and rollerball recaps was damning enough, but I believe it was Sparky's essence that threatened them most. You can't bottle charisma like his and dose it out in gel caps. As far as they're concerned, he was asking for it but good.

Massive riots broke out in this very wing last year. Windows were smashed. Fires were set. General pandemonium led to tear gas, heat rays and sound bullets to quash the rebellion. The entire administration was sacked.

The present administration is understandably paranoid about subversion on their watch. No doubt that's why they clamped down on Sparky with brutal force. We don't know what they did, but it was effective. When he returned to the bunkroom this evening after being detained for hours, there was very little spark visible in dear old Sparky. He just snoozed for hours like a sleepy bear with his face turned to the wall.

23 April

I held my breath, hoping against hope that Sparky was just grabbing a much-needed kip and would come 'round soon enough.

One by one, we stopped by his bunk to whisper encouragement, hoping he'd bounce back soon. When he finally awoke it was obvious that serious damage had occurred. Though he looked the same except for two small bruises on his temples and a dull glaze in his eyes, the nano-bite of personality Sparky displayed wouldn't have been a surprise puffing out of a mushroom.

He's adopted the zombie mope the rest of us had before his arrival: not talking and not caring. I've a feeling he won't be rising every morning to announce, "Ring the bell, lads! This day is meant for us alone." Won't be any more joining hands and marching around the bunkroom singing *Happy Days are Here Again*, either, now that a blanket's been wrapped tightly 'round Sparky's clapper.

Sparky's eyes looked cold as stones when I dared to look deep. When I try to chat he stares at the floor and mumbles incoherently. Just to make sure he's absolutely suppressed, they've got him on a massive programme of meds, "Necessary for therapeutic readjustment to community living," they say.

24 April

It shouldn't surprise us that Sparky wouldn't be allowed to stand. Seeing what's happened to him, we've reverted to good little zombies, greedily gulping meds we'd been flushing and spending our days drooling in front of the telly. It was all quite orderly; the last to emerge was the first to submerge.

Sparky is stuck in a black hole with the rest of us helplessly orbiting his event horizon. Seeing him like this sucks electrons off our last atoms of hope.

The second day after Sparky's treatment, I found Beddy's bongos cracked on the floor beside his bed. His face was turned to the wall. There was tension in his shoulders like he was suppressing sobs. Even the mighty Bedford Vann can only take so much.

"Oh well, we've still got Blancmange Thursdays," Stumpy sprinkled optimism over his eggs this morning.

"And there's 'the *Stu Bilat Show* every Saturday night." Bankrupt Bledsoe chimed in, spreading fake enthusiasm on his toast.

I chimed in, "Don't forget Wednesday afternoon papier-mâché' classes. I'm sculpting a life-size bust of Sparky."

Sparky's absence has sucked the oxygen out, leaving me uninterested in much beyond the telly. Does it embarrass me to spend countless hours watching turgid dramas, unreality shows, and mind-operas? Not really.

The authorities have ground Sparky's edges smooth enough to jam him into the hole where we all languished before he showed up. It's worse for us, having tasted freedom with Mr. Fuego's cheerleading, then having it revoked.

14 May

Miss Lilly has offered a shot at salvation. Said she can score me a halfway berth and an entry-level job with Teleternity if I stay the course. A change might do me good. Get back, honky cat. I'm on my way home.

I miss Jelly, my keytar, my porthole-equipped pad, and my trike. Perhaps with Lilly's help I can slide back to the old life and write "Up in Here I Raise A Lamp Beside the Golden Door to Explain the Mystery of Being" after all. Is that to be a poetry book? It's a dainty enough title for one. I don't know; it all seems over the horizon now.

Someone said good things come to the man who follows his plan, but I don't have a plan. According to William Blake this is dangerous, "He who desires but acts not, breeds pestilence."

Tomorrow, I act.

15 May
I was determined to write, but had an assignment to do first, so I sat at a library MemBrain and burned through two hours of Miss Lilly's *Course in Confidence*. Lessons on building self-pep were followed by an essay section, *How do thoughts become life's uploads?* It says obsessions can never be satisfied, leading to lockdowns at funny farms.

Free your mind and the rest will follow. I felt lighter reading that, but after straining my brain with coursework, I didn't feel like writing lyrics or compiling a quotes book. I felt knackered.

Returning to my bunk, I clamped on headphones, downloaded *The Zanti Misfits' Greatest Misses*, and fell asleep listening on repeat.

19 May
After grinding through Miss Lilly's *Course in Confidence*, I looked forward to her next visit.

"Hello, Mr. Fumbo." Miss Lilly sashayed in on a breeze of sandalwood, ocean spray and crabapples wearing a bronze metallic jumper and matching beanie with bug antennae.

She's a mysterious miss that I'm not getting through to as a man. Persian? Has a cute accent I can't place. A very *take care of business* type in any case.

"I checked results online and your test scores look very good indeed. Doctors are pleased, too. Based on your rapid progress, I'm recommending release to a halfway programme. Would you like that, Mr. Fumbo?" Her shiny, immaculately groomed, coal-black bob brushed about Miss Lilly's pretty, heart-shaped face as she spoke.

"Yes, at the earliest opportunity, please."

"Alright then, should be a breeze. This facility is overcrowded; they're looking to release as many guests as possible."

Accepting Miss Lilly's offer means binding my future to Teleternity, but if that's the road out, damn the torpedoes.

21 May / *London*
Due to my rapid success with her *Course in Confidence*,
Miss Lilly fulfilled her promise and sprung me to a halfway
house where I'm set to grope my way back to normal town.

22 May
Holding an entry-level job is a requirement for participation
in the halfway house programme. I've been assigned to sweep
the Snack Shack employees' cafeteria at the Teletemple as a
Sanitation Associate, Second Class where I'll earn creds that I'll
trade for crisps that I'll munch in my bunk.
   Haven't heard from Jelly in weeks. She's the kind of a girl
who makes the news of the world, so I wasn't surprised when
she popped up on telly coverage of a film premier, tumbling out
of a limo with fancy friends, all dressed up and laughing loud.
   "Hi!" The host greeted her.
   "Yeah, I am," Jelly slurred.
   I miss the old life at H-Block, but no worries, Miss Lilly
said there's some law that says they have to hold it for me. With
any luck, I'll be back gazing out my porthole at giant hologram
ladies and noodling on my keytar like nothing bad had ever
happened.
   I switched devices off and fell asleep.

24 May
Happy day! Sparky Fuego and Bedford Vann showed up
this morning, a miracle of early release due to overcrowded
facilities. Felt happy as Larry seeing the old Sparky is back, at
least most of the way. He hugged me so hard I could feel my
ribs shift position. Bedford Vann seemed the same as always,
just grunting, "Good to see ya, mate," as he shook my hand.
   "So, Fumbo" Sparky asked during lunch, "any progress on
your book?"
   "About to start on that."
   "What's it about again?"
   "A collection of wise quotes, densely-packed and indexed
for easy browsing, fresh from the vine and posted online. A tool
for living."
   "Nobody's got things figured out, do they?" Sparky sagged
at the thought.

"Don't believe they do. But some brilliant stabs have been made. A collection of those might sell."

"It's the unbearable lightness of being that bothers me," Sparky frowned. "We bluster about for eighty-odd years, then croak belly up. Loved ones mutter a few nice words and we're dust in the wind."

"Emerson said, If you would not be forgotten, either write things worth reading or do things worth writing."

"Well then, it's up to you to write something and make sure I'm remembered." Sparky smiled.

"Teleternists sanctify godcasts. Self-helpers chant homilies. Hindus meditate to levitate and Christians pray for the end of the world. Meanwhile, ancient wisdom lays buried in a grave marked *Neglect*. My book will raise those dusty words from the dead."

"Better get with it, before it backs up on you." Sparky's right. Must get off my arse and make it happen.

"A Teleternity expose' would sell tons. Can't believe no one's written one."

"Don't Telies have the juice to stop such efforts?" Sparky knew their reputation for playing legal defense.

"Quite possibly. Their rabid strategy is to tie opponents up in massive lawsuits 'til they cry uncle. They have the funds to do so. "

"Up in Here You'll Light a Fire And Blaze a Bright Path Through Life" could contrast philosophical quotes with the Telies' codswallop."

"Aren't we already numb from over-exposure to those dusty old quotes?" Sparky wanted to help, but I'd thought this through.

"Whether a single quote strikes a thunderbolt satori or the whole adds up to a general awakening, a condensation presented in bite-sized bits for modern attention spans could prove useful."

"Alright then, give us an sample?" Bedford joined in. It was good to hear him take an interest. I recited a favorite.

To see a world in a grain of sand
And heaven in a wild flower
Hold infinity in the palm of your hand
An eternity in an hour

"The micro reveals the macro—is that Blake's point?"

"I think he's saying the overall design is revealed in the tiniest bits as it is in massive ones; as above, so below—that's nature's way.".

I fell asleep and dreamed of Jelly lovin' super real. Got a great sex life; just wish I could be awake for some of it.

25 May

I went to the window where Nicotine Nic and Sparky enthused about a gorgeous rainbow arcing over the countryside in sunny spring rain. Standing there staring at its ephemeral beauty with my mates, I asked Sparky, "What's your view of heaven?"

"Heaven?" he looked perplexed, "Dunno really. What's yours?"

"I say heaven's here and now, we just need to wake up to it."

"Exactly how do you find that?" Sparky asked.

I pointed at the rainbow.

26 May

As I dumped a dustpan in the bin this morning, Miss Lilly O'Lilly ankled in, quivering with what looked like excitement in a checked peplum jacket and grey felt Robin Hood hat decorated with a pheasant's tail feather bouncing along in time with her prancing steps.

"Great news, Mr. Fumbo! It appears that your hard work has not gone unnoticed. In fact, your dedication to that linoleum has clearly established that you're ready for even greater responsibility. We're promoting you to counters wipe-down, effective immediately. Isn't this just the most exciting thing ever?"

"It is nice to have one's work recognized, Miss Lilly. But since I'm doing so well at sweeping, maybe I should stick with it?" I so enjoyed hearing Lilly's praise that I fudged in order to draw out more.

"Oh, Mr. Fumbo. I refuse to believe you're the type to stick with the tried and true, not with a fantastic promotion like this staring you in the face." Lilly's cheeks flushed with a passion I'd hadn't yet seen in her.

Does skillful sweeping excite Miss Lilly generally or is she just buzzed on my spectacular success with the Snack Shack floor? As I pondered this question, she shifted her posture slightly. Tilting her pelvis out, Lilly lowered her chin to look up at me through impossibly minky lashes and purr, "No one's ever made it from floor sweeper to counters wipe-down so quickly, Mr. Fumbo . . ." She grabbed both my hands and locked eyes with me. "No one . . . no one at all. Ever."

Crazy thoughts raced through my mind. Would Miss Lilly tumble for me if I accept this new position? Stu Bilat says women can't resist a man whose competence has not gone unrecognized.

Counters duty? Never in my wildest dreams did I dare to imagine it happening so fast. After all, as Miss Lilly pointed out, no one's ever made the jump so quickly.

It's dangerous assuming to know a lady's heart, but a certain sparkle in Miss Lilly's eyes told me she's impressed. Who am I to deny a lady her dream? Especially when that dream blows soft and warm like a quiet storm from the likes of Miss Lilly O'Lilly.

"So, Ignatius, what's your decision?" It was the first time she's used my Christian name. A reach for intimacy?

"Madam, I'll take it."

27 May
While wiping down acres of cold stainless steel in an empty cafeteria smelling of fried haddock, sanitizing cleanser, vinegar, and burnt toast, I spied an official-looking blue holdall propped up against a table leg. This was odd, as there hadn't been anyone around since I started the post-lunch wipe-down. No tag visible, so I cracked it open it to look for a clue. Inside its aromatic, leathery depths, I found a shiny silver bookchip with a glo-spine that read:

FOR YOUR EYES ONLY
TELETERNITY SECURITY
HIGHEST LEVEL
THE DIVINE COMEDY REVEALED

First thought: I should turn this over to my shift boss straightaway. Second thought: I need to suss this immediately.

I thought of slipping it under my shirt, but that's daft with CCTV everywhere. Hide in plain sight—that's the best way. I left the cafeteria carrying the hold-all openly like I was marching off to the authorities. Then I made a quick right turn in the hallway. There's no cams allowed in the loo. Safely locked in a stall, I uploaded it to my super-combi watch and promptly returned the case where I'd found it. James Bond keeps his mouth shut. That's the spy way.

Lying in my bunk at night, I projected the text on the wall next to me from my super-combi watch. My jaw dropped as I read the intro:

Extraterrestrials fine-tuned their DNA until they were able to live for a thousand years. This forced them to limit births, but despite their best efforts, their planet eventually became clogged with a vast, ancient population.

Lifespans of a thousand years brought centuries of time to kill. Bored to the point of insanity, they developed ever more gripping entertainments until a TV network jumped the competition by creating a reality show that planted life on other planets. This wasn't a challenge as they'd perfected warp tech and were able to travel immense distances in the blink of an eye. Probes were sent far and wide to discover new worlds able to support life. Robo spacecraft implanted suitable biology that was set to evolve at hyper speed while cams broadcast the fun live. The show proved wildly popular. So popular other networks felt challenged to invent even more elaborate concepts.

Finally they discovered a water planet placed third from its star, deeply endowed with resources and perfectly suited for life. Fiddling with the DNA of creatures they'd planted, the ancient ones sped evolution up so the leap to humankind happened with lightning speed.

Once they saw humans managing their affairs in groups, the aliens started to stir the pot in order to create drama. They invented different races, introduced the wheel to one lot, sailing craft to another, and astronomy to a third, just to watch the merry mix-ups. When wars broke out, they'd introduce advanced weaponry to one side and improved armor to the other. Bets were placed and heroes created with the cast never imagining they were merely actors strutting about for audiences a thousand light years distant.

They'd fling out a random upset and then track it forward and backwards in time, making small adjustments, playing it fast forward. Earth put on a cracking good show from caveman capers to the glories of ancient Egypt, European's arrival in the new word, oil-based economies rise and collapse, Foolish leaders strutted their stuff in high def 3D — and they were just the start. Soon after the Second World War, television producers revved up the earthling's technology by deliberately crashing a fake interplanetary craft in the New Mexican desert where Americans tested atom bombs. This became known as "The Roswell Incident."

The craft displayed technology just beyond earthlings' level, jump-starting the second half of their twentieth century with transistors, lasers, fiber optics, and computers.

If true, this means human history is just a series of ratings stunts and humankind exists as mere actors in a very long-running reality show. God is actually a telly producer siting in a darkened room, worried over ratings and humanity's struggles and strife are just light entertainment for ancient bags of bones somewhere deep in space.

Dear Diary, I was better off not knowing this. Are Teleternity priests the only ones beside me who are hip? If they suss what I suss, they'd drain me like puss. Or send my ass straight back to the mind-warp pavilion at Haversham's. Got to keep my head down and stay cool, all a geezer can do with a thing like this.

Could this be a cock-up by Teleternity? If so, why would they bother to test a humble janitor like me? Though admittedly, a janitor who's gone from floor sweeping to counter duty in record time. Did my rapid career advancement attract their attention?

The Telies are a sly bunch. They might have planted that hold-all on purpose, expecting me to ratfink them to a shocked world. They couldn't just call a press conference and announce something so massive, not when they're already seen as kooks.

Making the revelation seem like an unauthorized leak would lend credibility. Maybe it's a plot thickener, specifically designed to upset us for the amusement of the audience. People tend to believe things they're not supposed to know.

I just hope this mess doesn't stall my career momentum. Counters wipe-down is fine for now, but such rapid advancement has fired my ambition. Got my sights set on coffee brewing.

Yesterday my biggest challenge was scoring an extra pudding at lunch, and today I hold the biggest secret in all human history. Would have been better off handing the hold all over to lost and found without a peek.

My guess is that the TelePope is happy being thought of as a charlatan; that diverts attention, helping hide his secret. It also helps explain their obsession with television in general. Maybe they're holding it close to the vest in order to blackmail their way into the inner circles of power.

Pulled off my caper, but I'm in the dark about what to do next.

28 May

What can a poor boy do but play in a rock 'n roll band? This makes life a bitch when you don't have a band. Or even an instrument.

At lunch I asked Beddy if he was doing any music.

"Not really, but gotta hankering. You?"

"Always."

"Met a bloke at the Farm after you left. Plays any instrument you can name, sings, and produces, too." Beddy showed a side I'd never seen—something suspiciously like enthusiasm. "Name is Gearly. Wants to sit in with us."

The legendary Bedford Vann and I set up in a corner of the activity room and jammed on old standards. I hammered Casio chords over his bongo rhythms.

"Gearly and I jammed a bit after you left." Bedford offered by way of explanation.

"It shows."

Beddy didn't like my suggested name: The Blow Goes, but I think it'll grow on him.

Gearly baristas at an Orbit Espresso downtown, looks a lot like Che Guevara; drives a diesel van. Every band needs a front man, and a van. Bedford and I aren't the type to light ladies' dreams. Handsome Gearly's just what we need.

Beddy and I cut tracks on my MemBrain and emailed them to Gearly. He programmed bass, sweetened things, sang, and mixed it in 3D sound. They let him playlist our tunes at Orbit for customers to enjoy with their orange mocha frappuccinos. Sales are trending upwards.

New Music Echo interviewed us last week and today a UniCorp A&R man rang up hot to sign the Blow Goes to a global contract. But, as Bedford said, "Who wants to volunteer for slavery?" Beddy's got a tattoo, "DIY or DIE" inspired by his Black Mantas tragedy.

Blow Goes stack Brian Jones Pipes of Pan middle-eastern drones upside slap-back rockabilly echo with carnival-of-life lyrics weaving round sound effects set to throbbing Burundi beats echoed in deep reverb. A fresh sound shaded mysterioso by minor chord Mellotron strings and Theremin sighs Gearly lays on with surgical skill. I laid in bed buzzing, unable to sleep, thinking on things to come.

Our disturbed past has become a marketing hook. First article was headlined, "Blow Goes' Troubled Past Revealed." Fans eat our back-story like candy. And they're nutty for Tricky Dick. Our manager made a marketing icon out of Dick before we knew what he was up to. Fans are buying Tricky Dick logo wear like mad. Starting to feel like success is running away with us.

At least I hope things go like that. Dreamed up the italicized scenario, Dear Diary, every last bit. Miss Lilly's *Course in Confidence* has taught me to imagine things I want and screen a movie of it upside my melon. This is supposed to programme my subconscious while creating irresistible cosmic tractor beams that deliver the desired reality as if by magic. Can it really be that easy?

In reality, getting Gearly on board and choosing a band name is all that's happened so far, besides Beddy beating on an upended five-liter water bottle while I improvise beatnik lyrics and noodle on a dodgy Casio that's missing three keys. That's okay. We're woodshedding. Got hills to run up and things to shout before we stop for tea. It's cool like jazz.

29 May / *Blow Goes Cop a Lucky Break*
One of the halfway staffers is a Manta fan that knows Bedford's saga back to front. He's worked some loophole to provide us rental instruments as a therapy gambit. Beddy ordered our kit online.

Soon enough a van rolled up and unloaded like Christmas. Bedford scored a righteous drum kit with his favorite double bass. I'm sorted with a pearlescent-bodied keytar and practice amp. Gearly showed up to claim his sunburst hollow-body guitar, bass, synth, mixing deck and mics.

The Blow Goes are on.

After dinner we toasted our future over hot cups of peppermint tea and retired to an unused storage closet they've loaned us for rehearsals. We plugged in and bashed away, happy as idiots to be playing anything at all. Random buds of melody blooming amongst the weeds were all the encouragement we needed.

Beddy hasn't banged a proper kit in years, but it's obvious that he'll soon be whacking away at his old superstar level. Gearly's a solid pro on vocals, guitar, and mixing board—anything he picks up, I suspect. My limited keyboard chops place me in the front row of the marginally skilled. I'm lucky to be playing with this lot, but can't expect them to carry my weight.

30 May
Gearly has assumed the role of tech and set everything up good and proper. We jammed on some classics and kept things loose. It's a blast playing with these guys, even if their skill levels are far enough above me to be out of sight.

1 June
Beddy means business. Had us jam for eight hours
again today. We're making progress, but I'm still
lagging behind. Too knackered to write.

2 June
More practice—eight hours more.

3 June
See above.

4 June
Beddy enforces a soldier's discipline. We eat
breakfast, jam, stop for lunch, jam, have tea, jam some
more and keep at it 'til late at night. Our focus is intense.
Wrists and fingers complain, but they'll have to get used
to it.

5 June
"Can't expect brilliance from the start, but we're
coming along." Bedford spread encouragement on our
toast during breakfast. Nice that he said so, but I'm not
jamming good with him and Gearly.
"Worth another go," shouted Gearly at the end of a
new instrumental. Later, we got an ace groove on
executing *The Man Who Murdered Love*.

6 June
Beddy laid it down during breakfast, "Okay, lads.
Not there yet, but must press on regardless."
We bashed on into the night under the guidance of
the relentless Beddy. I did a little better, but my playing
still lags behind Beddy's tight-as-a-tick, rock-steady
grooves and Gearly's masterful playing.
Beddy called for a blues jam and we riffed an
endless *Spoonful*, followed by a thirty minute *Smoke on
The Water* that lit the sky.

7 June
Twelve hours of jamming has left me too knackered to write.

8 June
Today we tackled *Bedlam Bay*, a rocker Beddy wrote for the Black Mantas, never released due to legal wrangles. I was just happy to get through it without embarrassment. All the while I felt like an uncoordinated kid who is terrified the ball might come his way. It's becoming clear that I'm the weak link, but they'd never say so. Nobody wants to hold his mates back, least of all me.

9 June
More practice. Beddy decided it would be good to play for an audience, so we handed out flyers to our halfway housemates.

10 June
The Halfway Halfwitz, a wannabe comedy troupe of cracked actors who perform for fellow halfway guests were the only ones to show up and watch us rehearse.

Just after lunch twenty troubled souls crouched on bare concrete looking up at us like they were expecting the answer to a question they couldn't quite frame.

We laid on a heaping *Spoonful* and got hung up on that riff again. After twenty minutes of spoonful, spoonful, spoonful, audience members began to slip out the exit, but we'd caught a groove and couldn't let go.

Halfway through *Bedlam Bay*, Beddy nodded for me to take a lead. I tapped my effects panel, racing through options from wah-wah to StarMonizer, masking my simple-minded chording with a catalog of distortions. Might have overused the StarMonizer a bit, I saw Gearly wince a couple times.

We bashed on, drilling our audience deep into The Blow Goes' sound, whatever that is. At the end, those who were able to do so rose to give us a standing ovation. I caught Beddy grinning; he was dead chuffed at their reaction.

"I'd like to say thank you on behalf of myself and the group and I hope we passed the audition." Gearly dismissed the audience with Lennon's goodbye from the rooftop.

It's increasingly obvious I'm not playing at the others' level. An honest review of our performance might read: *800-Pound Gorilla Stinks Up Stage And No One Mentions It.*

12 June

Beddy is proving to be quite serious about this band of misfits. Played for another eight hours today. Things are tightening up, but I'm holding them back. Being a drag is a drag. I brought it up to Beddy during breakfast. "Can't go 'round the world in a day," he shrugged it off.

13 June

Rehearsed nonstop again. We're jelling as a band despite the fact my chops lag behind the others'.

This morning I asked Beddy if he felt like a cuppa. He said okay and we copped a booth at a Rapido. "Sorry to rain on this parade," I said, "But, fact is, I haven't got the chops of you and Gearly. I'm holding things back and you know it."

Beddy thought for a moment before speaking, "Gotta brass your bollocks, mate. We're a three-piece and a tripod can't stand on two legs. You're not holding us back. Your lyrics are brilliant; they inspire us. Your playing is adequate and you'll get better. There's no band without all three of us. So, no more such talk or I'll leave you lot, meself."

No one can disagree when Bedford Vann lays it down like that. I was flattered to hear the longest speech ever from him, but had to wonder if he's considering the band's success or just being loyal to a mate.

14 June

I showed the boys a fresh lyric called *Brighton Sands*. Gearly had a chunky mid-tempo groove he wanted to try. We had a bash and found his chords wrapped around my words nicely. He added effects, banged out a rough mix, and we had something cool.

A girl blurred by in London
Another in Cologne
Faces in the rain
Seen from a train
On Brighton sands
We sang this song,
We sang it all night long
On Brighton sands
We sang
Everything we see is ours forever
Only you and me
See snow when it's rain
And pleasure when it's pain
And share a pair of eyes
Staring in surprise
That everything we see is ours forever

Tried to keep up, but my fingers cramped and I had to stop. Threw the others off and we halted cold, spoiling the moment.

Gearly and Beddy took off on a shuffle beat thing Gearly wrote and really got it on. Sounds like a hit. He called it *Pretty Dirty* and was so chuffed, he said he'd contact Major Boyle, a top manager he knows from his last band.

Gearly talked Beddy into an online release. The Blow Goes are officially out in the world as a recording act(!)

15 June

We met for lunch with Major Boyle and hired him on the spot. Gearly had sent demos that he's mad about. Boyle swears he can put us over and we believe him. He was Johnny Zhivago's original manager, after all. Having him on our team massively pumps up confidence all around.

Our jam today went better than ever, at least for the others. I stumbled a bit. They were forgiving, but I felt lame.

16 June

Practice. Practice. Practice. Bedford and Gearly really flew today, playing such hot synch grooves that I struggled to keep up. Plodding along, choking on their dust was the best I could manage, faking it when I couldn't make it. They knew what I was doing, but didn't say a thing.

Gearly records everything we do and says he's copping grooves he can sculpt into hits. Bummed me when I caught him re-doing one of my parts.

17 June
Awoke from a nightmare: we were playing a massive venue with thousands of fans at our feet. I froze solid and couldn't play a note. A portent? I'd hoped my chops would tighten with practice, but that's not happening fast enough. The others are getting better faster than I am, a disturbing trend.

Beddy's too loyal to say anything and Gearly isn't the type to point fingers.

What's the obvious solution? I have to split. If I leave they'll find a better keyboardist and The Blow Goes will be on their way to the toppermost of the poppermost where they belong. Beddy doesn't need a wanker like me holding back his comeback, but he'd never accept my resignation. The solution? I've got to go. Some time away will help me sort things.

18 June
So never refuse an invitation, never resist the unfamiliar, never fail to be polite and never outstay the welcome. Just keep your mind open and suck in the experience. And if it hurts, you know what? It's probably worth it.
- Jack Kerouac

I stuffed a gob of clothes and snacks and snuck out through the bathroom window as everyone slept in blissful unawareness of my treachery.

I'm a long gone daddy, but where to?

Figuring some sea air might clear the smog from my noggin, I took the Underground to Victoria Station and bought a ticket to Brighton. Not having ridden a train since my crack-up, I was eager to get on with it, but there were no Brighton runs 'til 8am. Finally scored a window seat and settled in to watch London roll by to a clickety-clack click-track.

I'm officially an escapee.

A smallish bloke with milk-white Irish skin, wavy ginger hair, and a chin beard that formed a ring 'round his face like a fur-covered toilet seat, sat down opposite me. Going by stenciled lettering running down the sleeve of his rough-sewn olive-coloured canvas jacket: *Who Misses the Grid?* I judged him to be an *offy*.

We chatted amiably. When I mentioned my rootlessness, Nigel invited me to grab a night's kip at his commune just outside Brighton. Might be a dodgy scheme, but free lodgings don't come cheap. Probably better to hide amongst a group of offies instead of standing out like a runaway.

Nigel wore olive-drab ankle-length trousers with too many pockets, a collarless shirt, and a beige plastic pith helmet with a red-tipped antenna that bounced while he talked. Mirrored space shades glittered from a macramé lanyard around his neck and a bloom of spidery metal tools sprouted from a shirt pocket. He looked equipped for anything as he fidgeted for snack in an onboard storage pouch, leaned back and savored carbo bliss. His hat tipped up when its brim hit the seatback, like a silent comedian's bit. I laughed. Nigel repeated the trick and laughed too. A queenly-looking middle-aged lady next to him didn't see the humour. Neither did the sullen teen with jet-black hair and ivory skin engrossed in an NME cover story on Death Row Jethro's posthumous album.

Speeding into a darkened tunnel, I sat waiting for light to appear on the other side. Out of the tunnel and into the landscape, Nigel pointed out sights, explaining why they loom large in legend.

In less than an hour we pulled into the drab, crumbling Brighton station decaying under a soggy grey sky that wouldn't rain, but wasn't about to give up on the idea. Nigel said a mate would pick us up, "I texted ahead. They're looking forward to meeting you."

"Just so long as you don't try to recruit me."

"No worries mate. We don't want reluctant recruits."

We waited in the pick-up lane 'til a clapped-out van with an observation blister on its roof pulled up with a clatter and squeak. A tanned, freckle-faced girl with a bright smile, lush brows, and wavy strawberry hair swung out a squeaky door.

"A'lo sailors!" she called.

We piled in. Nigel introduced me to Jess. She shook my hand and grabbed the wheel to horse that rickety crate onto the motorway. Three of us were crammed onto the single seat, swaying left and right like bobble heads as Jess took the curves like a Formula One ace. The van's struts were blown, so it swayed like a boat in a side swell. I felt carsick and rolled down a window. A blast of salt air hit my face, smelling like freedom.

Jess clicked the radio onto a gospel punk station, *Who Waters the Lawns of Heaven?* Played softly.

"Love this." Jess exclaimed, turning up the volume.
Who, tell me who
Waters the lawns of heaven?
Would it be me?
Could it be you?
Tell me who,
Who waters the lawns of heaven
With their tears?

"Shinky that you still get radio here."

"It's our own station," Nigel beamed with pride.

We pulled up to a ragged huddle of scrap-built domes, homemade wind turbines, rainwater collectors, and jury-rigged solar cells. A towering wicker statue of a female figure wearing a crown of leaves glared down on the compound with glowing green eyes. A few suede-headed kids played beside a well-tended vegetable garden stretching for acres with beehives scattered about with a row of white-framed greenhouses occupying the middle distance. Goats munched in a pen. Chickens scratched about. Everything looked sorted, especially given the offies' reputation as lay-abouts.

"Good timing, lads." Jess commented, "Lunch in fifteen."

We passed biomass generators feeding fat power lines leading to a copper-clad dome sparkling at the end of an alley of energy.

At noontime we all filed into the copper dome where we were bathed in rays of amber light from tinted

Perspex bubbles dotted about. A large, round, wooden table dominated an open space where I sat between Nigel and Jess in a sturdy, homemade chair. Nigel stood, motioned for me to do the same and introduced me to everyone. Each stood in turn and repeated my name as they clasped their hands in prayer. Felt a bit creepy.

A middle-aged lady with steely grey hair arranged in a puffy bun rolled up a cart piled high with a strange-looking green mash. Nigel caught my puzzled look, "Bug protein, bee pollen, fresh greens, seaweed, coconut oil, and whatever's ripe in the garden. Gives you big energy to do big things." He noticed my skeptical look and added, "It's not as bad as it looks. You'll get used to it." Didn't mention that I won't be around long enough for that.

The offies seem cool, if a bit Stepford.

Leaving the dining hall, I spotted an old upright piano, sat down, and pounded some boogie-woogie. A small crowd of offies gathered about, listening raptly and clapping along. I played three songs and held them spellbound. They broke out enthusiastic applause when I stopped. Playing for an audience felt like a quenching cup of water to a man thirsting for his art.

19 June

An arsehole rooster woke me far too early, but the worse was yet to come when Nigel appeared at the tent flap to announce a mandatory workout. It seemed their domed dining hall doubles as gymnasium

Jumping, jogging, touching toes, jumping jacks, and stretches left me starving for breakfast.

I sat with Jess and Nigel for eggs, tomato slices, apple juice and whole grain toast with goat butter and homemade jam. Jess explained, "Everything is grown or made on site."

There's always a hidden cost with a lot like this. No doubt I'll find that out later.

Jess suggested a trike ride to the beach. I hadn't seen it since long ago family holidays and was eager to take a look. We pedaled through a warm, damp breeze on what she described as "Franken-trikes cobbled together from trash bin parts." As we pedaled toward Albion's fair shore, a couple decked in perfect mod gear buzzed by on a bedazzled Vespa scooter.

A few miles ride brought us to Brighton's crumbling pier. The half that wasn't swamped was washed away. It made me sad, thinking on happy times spent there with mum and dad. All that remained of the beach was a narrow strip hugging the rising sea like a last stand for all that went before.

Jess's eyes sparkled a deep green that reflected the sea. As we strolled the narrow beach looking out at endless ocean, the ends of the earth didn't seem that far to go. We spied a private spot and Jess pulled a blanket from her pack. We stripped to what was underneath and laid down to soak up hot sun.

Jess turned to say, "Why are you rambling about aimlessly?"

I was tired of telling my tale and hesitated to answer.

"I like to hear people's stories," she prodded, "what's yours?"

"Just starting a career as a stray dog. Reckon I'll wander about 'til I run into something good. My only question is where to next?"

"Would you consider joining us?"

"It'd be easy to get used to this, but I'm not a joiner."

"Every day can't be a holiday." As much as I liked Jess, I suspected this lovely idyl was but a ruse intended to hook me into their cultish clutches. All too soon I wouldn't be hanging out on a beach with a gorgeous bird, but rising at dawn to slop hogs and shovel manure.

I listened to wild-sounding gulls' calls complemented by ocean's roar and something that sounded like distant thunder.

Jess leaned over and kissed me, more passionately than before. We made love on the sand and lay side-by-side soaking up sunrays that felt like a hot balm. I wanted to run into the sea and baptize myself. I loved everything because everything was good and doing the best it could.

Closing my eyes, I drifted off to dreamland.

Then I awoke.

Is this some kind of joke?

I was alone. This bird had flown. An on-shore breeze dusted me with a uniform coating of sand. The sun had sunk without a trace, leaving a million stars flickering above. Where was my angel of the morning?

Our trikes were still parked where we'd left them. Was she taking a swim? A few geezers splashed in the sea. I walked down to have a look and kept on straight into the water. Shivering at first, I kept on 'til it was waist deep and dove under incoming waves to avoid their battering. They lifted me and let me down in gentle swells that pressed on to die at the shore. Bathing in that immense, cold ocean made my little worries seem very small indeed. I popped to the surface to float on my back staring at puffy clouds floating by in darkening twilight. I remembered Cathode Ray's quote from t.s. eliot, *For whatever we lose (like a you or a me) it's always ourselves we find in the sea.*

Something tugged violently at my right foot. Instantly panicked, I thrashed about trying to kick free of a monster that saw me as dinner. I had no luck; it held fast. Twisting about in order to face my attacker, I saw Jess release my leg, smiling broadly as she let go and bobbed to the surface.

"You bastard!" I shouted. She laughed. We swam 'til our feet touched bottom, then walked to the beach holding hands. With her face framed by dripping wet hair in the moonlight, Jess looked more beautiful than ever.

"Where were you off to?"

"You were snoring too loud for me to think. Didn't want to disturb you so I took a long walk." She laughed.

"What now?"

"We need to get back. They'll start to wonder if I've kidnapped you. Besides, it's dinner time."

Arriving out of breath from our hot pedal up the coast, we parked the trikes and made our way to the dining hall for fresh greens, homemade wine, and catch of the day. Their leader Jacob asked to speak with me afterwards. Sitting on a bench overlooking the moonlit sea, he smiled and asked, "How do you like our settlement?"

"All seems quite sorted. Impressive how you've worked out the self-sufficiency everyone's striving for."

"It's been a steep mountain to climb and we made every mistake in the book, but we're not done yet—and never will be. That'd be boring."

Jacob turned serious, "Have any questions?"

"Not really. I've had a lovely time, but I'll be moving along soon. I want to thank you all for the hospitality."

"Sorry to hear that. We'd hoped you'd hang on long enough to see if you fit."

"Most grateful for everything."

"Well, good luck. If you've any questions, I'm around."

20 June

I snuck from the tent at dawn and crept to the kitchen where I nicked a chunk of cheese, an apple, and half a baguette, and left a note:

Thanks a million for your hospitality. Though I admire your accomplishments and appreciate the kindness you showed me, my future lies elsewhere.

Cheers,

I. Fumbo

And so I struck off down the mysterious roads of Albion once again, thinking about visiting Southampton as a bustling seaport might offer employment.

Made my way to the motorway and stuck my thumb out at tiny self-guided electric pods whooshing by in coupled trains of five to ten. Drivers stared at screens, grimly determined not to make eye contact with a roadside drifter.

After an hour I grew discouraged and walking in search of a better spot, found a lorry pullout after a mile or so. Soon enough, the sharp blast of an air horn nearly startled me out of my Chelsea boots. I turned 'round and saw a lorry pulling up with its minder motioning to me from behind a tall windscreen. I ran over and hopped inside. It was warm and cosy, smelling faintly of cinnamon and a musky animal essence. Hank Williams crooned lonesome country blues softly in ambi-sound.

The driver extended his hand for a shake, "Declan here, where ye headed, then?"

"Ignatius Fumbo. Southampton sounds good. And you?"

"Southampton's the ticket. I'm one of the few left to load at their docks."

Declan was burly with a ruddy face, curly salt and pepper hair, and thick beard, a jolly, working man type.

"Why are you going there?"

"Just meandering about, really. Thought I'd have a look."

"Fleeing something?"

"In a way, yeah. Nothing criminal."

"Not one to judge. Seen me own rambles."

"I was rehearsing with a little band. We had some lucky connections and it was looking like we might make it, but I wasn't pulling my weight. Didn't think it fair to hold them back, so I split."

"But if they're happy with you, maybe that bit's all in your head?"

"Don't think so."

Declan left the rig on autopilot as we motored along to the soothing caress of pedal steel guitars stroked by long gone honky-tonk heroes.

"Care for a nip? Sailors' rum." Declan handed me a hammered nickel flask. I took a pull of high-octane, shuddered, and handed it back. He did the same, but without the shuddering. A second round warmed me up nicely.

"And how's about one for Tricky Dick?" Declan reached behind his head and pulled open a curtain on a compartment where a bored-looking rhesus monkey sat wearing a red kerchief and porkpie hat set at a jaunty angle. Seeing the flask got him hopping about with excitement.

"He's a funny geezer, that Tricky Dick. Likes a nip."

Declan slid open the partition, gave Dick a gulp of spirits and freed him to roam about the cab. The hairy beast climbed up on my shoulder for a peak out the windscreen. So close, I felt his hot rum breath on my neck. Declan spoke, "Dick takes a fancy to very few people but he seems to like you."

The song ended and a geezer came on to spew politics like they mattered. *A corrupt government leads its citizens into a dark canyon of cynicism. Deep in those sunless depths, decay sets in and strange fungi grow fat feeding off the rotting corpse of the body politic*

Declan addressed the radio, "Sound and fury, signifying nothing."

SMASH!

Something massive struck the cab's roof. I slid down in my seat to avoid injury as the ceiling caved in like a smashed tin of beans.

Tricky Dick screeched and jumped into my lap.

Choking smoke poured into the cab as we smashed a guardrail.

The lorry skidded into a full-circle spin, smacked a power pole, and bashed in Declan's door, rolling the huge rig over onto its side. Suspended on the high side by my seatbelt, I unbuckled, grabbed Dick, and climbed over Declan who looked out cold. Leaving the monkey beside the road, I climbed back inside and checked Declan for a pulse. Nothing showing.

Leaned down to see if he was breathing, no hope there, either. Under-dash wires crackled and sparked as a smoldering electrical stench choked off my breath.

Pulled Declan from the smoky cab and drug his heavy body with his boot heels serving as skids. Once we were far enough to be safe, I laid him down with his jacket for a pillow and checked his vitals. Got the same reading, so I straddled him and administered CPR, forcing air into his lungs with everything I had. Nothing happened. I gave up and shoved mightily on his chest. Checked his pulse again. No luck. Finally, I drug him down the motorway a bit farther and propped him up against a guardrail so he'd be easily spotted.

Fire burst from the lorry, exploding into a fireball that consumed the entire rig in a ball of flame. Grabbing Dick's hand, I ran across the motorway as fast as I could before stopping to check out the mess of shiny metal contorted as if in agony. Cracked-up solar cells and sparking wires hissing like electric snakes were embedded in the smashed cab.

Space junk.

There was nothing to do for Declan so I sprinted down the motorway holding Tricky Dick's hand. A police car flew toward the wreck at top speed, followed by a fire engine and ambulance.

I walked a few miles holding my thumb out at uncaring traffic. Eventually a *Spyder Trike* driven by a lovely Asian miss pulled up and Tricky Dick climbed in without waiting for an invitation.

"Hi, I'm Kathy Fong."

Kathy Fong was the bomb, a raven-haired, Chinese beauty turned out in false eyelashes, pencil skirt, and tilted mini-top hat with blinking antennae.

"Thanks so much for stopping; I'm Ignatius Fumbo."

She extended a delicate, perfectly manicured hand. I extended my grubby mitt and we shook.

"Do you always travel with a monkey?"

"My first day, actually."

Kathy Fong arced a perfect brow over eyes lit up brilliant golden orange by a dying sun.

"I was in a horrific accident just now."

"Really? What happened?"

"Space junk smashed the cab of a lorry I'd hitched a ride in, killing its minder. This is his monkey; had no choice but to adopt him."

"Sorry. You must be shook."

"It's not about me."

"Got something that might prove a healthy distraction."

"Really?"

"Ever sex-synched, Fumbo? Might be just what you need." Kathy Fong's mild buckteeth rested softly on her pink, pillowy lips like sexy pearls.

"Sex-synched?"

"Yes—synchronized group orgasms."

"Heard of it, but no, never tried."

"Want to try, English boy?"

Kathy's invitation rattled my already shaky cage.

"Headed to a pit now, actually. I've never introduced a newbie, you'll be my first victim." Kathy Fong laughed wildly. She weirded me out and randied me up in equal measure.

"What else do you do?"

"I tend tanks at a hydro-farm. Pays the bills, but coincidentally enough, I'm training to become a space junk impact site investigator. And you?"

"I'm a fugitive from a band on the run."

"How's that?"

"I was playing music with some mates, but things weren't right. Had to split and sort things."

"Sorters welcome here."

"So what's synchronized orgasm like?"

Graphic for a Blow Goes single release

WHITE TRASH
AND I'M PROUD

Blow Goes album cover

SPYDER TRIKE

Tricky Dick merchandise logo

"If you can hold out, you'll orgasm in synch with a roomful of punters, booting a shot of orgone energy that's impossible to describe. And just as impossible to forget. You don't have to worry, everyone's been checked and certified."

Electronic bat cries, boogie-woogie bass lines, and Theremin whines filled the night with sexy menace as, just off a country lane, we came to a ribbed-metal half-cylinder laid on its side. I grabbed a blanket and made a bed for Tricky Dick, but first took a walk and let him do his thing. When we returned, Kathy Fong gave Dick a water bottle he greedily sucked like a baby. Must remember to hydrate the monkey.

Kathy Fong flashed her embed at a tuxedo clad doorwoman and led me to a nurse for a quick check up. We entered the dark cylinder lit by flickering amber lights shimmering on ribbed metal walls. The room buzzed with sexual energy, but after what had happened to Declan, I wasn't in the mood. Then Kathy Fong snuggled up and other thoughts occurred.

Hot new Indian pop star Cintra crooned *Caveman Love* from her *Songs for Sonoramic Commandos* album over a hypnotic beat as illuminated holos of sex, salvation, and spanking flickered on curved aluminum walls.

Caveman love
That's what we're made of
'Cause caveman love
Comes from above
So that's what we're made of
We're made of caveman love

"Syncro-gasm in half an hour, Fumbo. Do yourself a favour and hold out for it. I'll join you so we can come together. A five-minute alert will be followed by another every minute until the final minute counts down in seconds. Get it?"

"Got it."

"Good."

"Sorry, Kathy. I'm not up for this. My mood ring's spun dead black."

"What's that mean?"

"A good man died in my arms."

Kathy Fong kissed my cheek and purred in my ear, "Don't worry, baby. You can wait in the trike. We'll talk after." She gave my thigh a squeeze and walked away.

So, instead of making love to a delicate lotus blossom in a steamy sex pit, I sat in her trike reading a strange little book on ancient aliens I found in a map pocket.

I took Tricky Dick for a walk, returned to her trike, reclined the seat and tried to nap. Had no luck so I went back to reading. After a bit, Kathy Fong emerged from the sex-tube with a glazed look and wan smile.

"My, that was refreshing." She said, stoned, blissful, and spent.

"I've gotta find a place to sleep." The chilly, damp coastal air had inspired hope that Miss Fong would offer lodgings.

"Sorry, can't help with that, living with my parents."

"No worries. I'll be off then. Ciao." We kissed like brother and sister.

Dick and I set off to haunt lonely roads once again, passing cosy-looking houses that looked like boxes filled with love and caring.

After an hour's trudge, I spied a weather-beaten sign that read *Cock & Bull* over the door of a crumbly old pub. I stepped inside its dimly lit interior holding Tricky Dick's hand. He looked up, shooting me an expression like, "I hope you know what you're doing."

Well-fortified cheery locals huddled around an upright piano braying trad songs at alcoholic volume. They turned as one to look at us, did a double take at Dick, and returned to their bellowing.

I ordered a pint of Guinness from a cherubic barmaid with a ready smile, NHS glasses, and a porcelain complexion. I tossed the malty brew down and felt better instantly. Left a bit in the glass I handed off to Tricky Dick when no one was looking. He gulped it with great relish.

The tone-deaf chorus finished pummeling their songbook and retired to their tables. After a third round of Guinness I felt ready to approach the piano and pound out Beddy's *Bedlam Bay*. A lanky, twenty-something brunette with one eye hidden behind a sexy drape of hair, sauntered over and hummed along. When I finished with a flourish she smiled and said, "What's that? Sounds Black Manta-ish."

"Very astute, it's an unreleased song of theirs."

"Mind if I sit in? I'm Lulu." She extended a hand. I felt the curse of the lonely beatnik lift when I looked into Lulu's soft brown eyes.

"Ignatius Fumbo."

We shook on it.

"Live around here?" I cocked an eyebrow in a wise guy expression. She laughed.

"Yup. You?"

"On holiday from nowhere."

"Well, I can dig it."

"Know of any cheap lodgings about?"

"Is free cheap enough?"

"That would do nicely."

"My brother's out of town so we've a free bed. Could be your break, but first, let's play some more tunes. "

We rampaged through what I knew of the Mantas' catalog with Tricky Dick beside us, swaying to the music, totally absorbed. At least, I thought he was until he hopped off the bench and scampered about, copping the dregs of abandoned pints. He soon got wobbly and I suggested we leave.

Lulu lit up her family's pearl-white Humber Electro and drove me to a thatched-roof cottage set in a deep forest glade lit by dappled moonlight. It looked magical, like a storybook. She introduced mum and dad, who were bedecked in gaily-printed matching pyjamas. They liked Tricky Dick and he seemed to enjoy their attention between his random burps and drunken squeals.

I felt like a subtle astronaut looking down on a beautiful world he could never quite reach, a world where sweet, down-to-earth Lulu lives in a woodsy glade with her sweet, down-to-earth family and nothing bad could ever happen.

"Thirsty Puppy plays in town tonight." Lulu said, hiking her white moon breasts up high and round.

"Never seen 'em."

"Want to?"

"Bossa nova, baby."

Things were shaping up nicely all around.

Lulu relit the Humber and we motored to a club called No Regrets where Thirsty Puppy played hard and soft all night long, mostly songs from their third album *Tidal Pool Cues*.

Anything that draws blood
Is not invisible
This message understood
Her foray successful
She'd paid her dues
She paid 'em with the tidal blues
There beside the sea
She said this to me
I paid my dues
I paid 'em with the tidal blues

Afterwards, motoring along in Lulu's silent electric car, her enchanting display of cleavage inspired me to wonder if I had a chance. She must have sensed my thought, "Too bad my boyfriend is out of town. I think you two would get on."

Boyfriend.

I slept in her brother's room with Tricky Dick snoring like a monster at the foot of the bed.

21 June / *A bird without a perch must keep flying.*

I enjoyed a lovely breakfast of eggs, beans, and bangers with the family and promptly hit the road to Southampton.

Tricky Dick has proven quite a good traveler, bobbing along quietly in my backpack, checking things out like a born tourist. And motorists no longer avert their eyes when I stick out my thumb. Now they gape at a thing with two heads.

After an hour's wait, I caught a ride with a middle-aged accountant named Buster driving a bully pod with air-cooling seats. I reckoned anyone willing to pick up a geezer traveling with a monkey would show a bit of personality, but I wasn't able to detect any such emission from Buster.

A dead quiet ride down the motorway brought us to a Rapido for lunch where we ate in silence broken only by chewing and sipping sounds.

Buster let me off at the edge of Southampton beneath a sign that boasted. *Historic sailing port of the Mayflower and Titanic*. He pointed at it and said, "One out of two isn't bad." He'd busted out a joke at last, just before wishing me, "Good luck," as I stepped out of his pod and into my next adventure.

Thought I might find a boat needing hands and ship out for shores unknown. But, on second thought, they probably don't allow monkeys unless you're a pirate. Maybe I could load cargo on the docks? Too knackered to do any research, I found a hostel and flopped.

Writing this in my bunk. They allow pets here, but locked poor Dick in a smelly basement with a bunch of nervous mutts barking their fool heads off. I regret sticking him in there, but it's just for a night. I'll find something better in the morning. Thoroughly knackered, I nodded out instantly.

I awoke to a panicked innkeeper shouting in my ear.

"Mr. Fumbo, wake up, sir! Please, sir! Wake up!" He shouted, "Your monkey's loose! Loose, I tell you!"

Allowed free reign to search the premises, I checked closets, bedrooms, and attic while calling his name. He was nowhere to be found. "Not funny, Dick," I sputtered.

I heard a clatter from the kitchen. As I stood there, figuring my next move, Dick stuck his furry little head out from behind a pantry door. His mug was smeared with whipped cream like he was ready to shave. As he pointed a banana at me like a gun, I heard a pan clatter to the floor behind him. The floor was covered with flour piled up like snow on the broken china and spilled beans. I took Dick's hand, grabbed my pack, and quietly slipped out the back. We strode briskly to the docks where I had a mind to look for a ship that's hiring.

I felt insignificant standing in the deep shadows beside those mighty steel leviathans. One thing was clear, giant merchant ships do not hang Help Wanted signs off their poop decks. I needed street level info.

Turning a corner, I spotted a crusty looking sea dog sitting on a crate, strumming a ukulele, and singing in a gravely Popeye voice. A few cred-coins glittered in a worn yachting cap upturned on the sidewalk.

My beautiful,
Dutiful mermaid

As he sang, Tricky Dick jumped into my arms. I held him as we listened.

On and on, under the sea she swam
On and on under the sea
She swam and swam, my fin-tailed sham
My mermaid swam
My beautiful
Dutiful mermaid

A song by Eddie Mort I recognized.

Tricky Dick seemed fascinated.

"Lovely song." I said.

"Say it with cash." He croaked.

"Sorry, haven't any coins. Know any ships that are hiring?"

He laughed and shook his head. "Haven't a clue, do ya?"

"What do you mean?"

"Dinosaurs." He said, gesturing toward the ominous hulks towering overhead. "Do they look like they're going anywhere?"

"They look more likely to sink than sail."

"No demand for goods when nobody's got a quid to spend. So, there's no shipping. There are very few jobs in a graveyard. You best look for work elsewhere."

He looked me up and down.

"On the run, are ya?"

"I must be shouting it. Nothing illegal."

"Well if you'll kindly buy an old salt a pint, I'll be glad to shed a light on your local options."

"Lead the way." Didn't have extra creds to throw around on drinks, but I was desperate.

He stuck his hand out for a shake.

"Nichol. Jimmy Nichol."

"Ignatius Fumbo." We shook on it.

Jimmy grabbed Tricky Dick's hand and shook it gently.

We walked to The Sandpiper, a dim pub smelling of
cigarettes, stale pints, and hopelessness with every seat
filled but two at the end of the bar. "They're expecting
us," croaked Jimmy. I pointed at the monkey and the
bartender nodded okay.

We ordered two Guinness from a flirty brunette in a
tight-fitting naval suit.

"So, you've sailed the seven seas?" I was keen to
hear some salty dog tales.

"So I did. Then came the bad times and I didn't.
What brings you here?"

"As you guessed, I'm escaping. Some mates and I
started a band, but my lack of skill was holding them
back, though they wouldn't admit it."

"Maybe you helped them in ways more important
than technical skill. Don't fight the magic."

I spied Dick cosying up in the lap of a bosomy
matron draining a pint with gusto. She gulped, belched,
and smiled down at the wee ape like he was her very
own babe in arms.

I tried to grab Dick and drag him off her lap, but he
wouldn't budge.

"Don't take my baby!" she seemed only half
kidding.

"Why do you travel with a monkey, anyway?" She
slurred.

"A forced adoption, we mobbed up on the road."

"Well, he's just the cutest thing ever."

I walked Dick back to Jimmy. "Needing somewhere
to grab a kip. Any options?"

"There are options." He said.

He drained his glass and offered advice, "My hunch
is that you belong in that band, mate. They'll decide
who's in and who's out. You're hurting them by bailing.
It's your grand chance. And you're a fool if you blow it
out of some misplaced sense of nobility."

Appreciated his advice, but that option didn't fit my
plan. I didn't even fit my plan.

"You have a point." I smiled at Jimmy.

"Life's short. A geezer doesn't get many lucky
breaks. Shakespeare said there's a tide in the affairs of

men. Gotta grab it at the full or stand there and get your shoes wet. Sounds like your tide's in with this band."

Dick and I flopped at a decrepit hotel Jimmy recommended. Not many salts about these days so they were happy to see us. Rooms were dirt-cheap and the frowsy, bleached-blond desk clerk didn't care if Dick shared mine. She didn't seem to care about anything beyond her next ciggy.

Dick and I lay atop a scratchy wool blanket, Jimmy's words echoing in my melon as I stared up at the ceiling, unable to sleep. Tricky Dick stared at me as I racked my brain looking for a flaw in Jimmy's advice, but had no luck.

22 June

Woke up thinking that Jimmy's advice is right. Beddy and Gearly will be worried. I've been a right twit.

I texted them both: *Sorry for the disappearing act. I'm okay, really. Just sorting things, is all.*

Situation inventory:
1. Sailing the seas? Not happening.
2. Creds? Slim to disappearing.
3. Monkey pal? Deserves a stable situation.

Tricky Dick and I took breakfast at a dodgy seaman's café just off the quay. There was no one about but a lonely counterman with a hangdog face singing along to a sad country song playing from a cheap plastic radio. He seemed to brighten a little, seeing us. I had beans and toast. Dick inhaled a banana, so I bought him two more.

MemBrain buzzed with a text from Beddy:
Glad to hear you're well.
Kindly suggest you get your skinny ass back here immediately or I'll make you wish you had.
Always your drummer,
Bedford

Nice to see his text, but I'd still be a drag on their wheels. Should I man up and face the music I'm barely able to make? Or just wander about until I discover signs of life somewhere?

With a mind blank as slate, I zombie-walked to the depot and bought a ticket for Victoria Station. Not sure about returning to London. Dick seems jumpy too.

I spied a bench and sat down across from an impeccably dressed older gent with steel grey, shoulder-length hair framing a wise-looking face bearing a wispy goatee and wry half-smile. He looked vaguely Asian, an impression furthered by his mandarin-collared, silver sharkskin suit.

He unrolled a MemBrain and impatiently scrolled its screen, hovering in the air between us. Seemingly upset, he rolled it up and stared straight through me for an ice-cold second before saying, "Who sent you?" while gazing fixedly through gun-slit eyes.

"No one sent me. What's the panic?"

"Professor Emeritus Nathan Freebinder. Forgive me for suspecting you, but I can't be too careful."

"Why would anyone stalk you?"

"I've hatched a plan to save the world from over crowding. But such a paradigm-shifting strategy threatens the powers that be. They'll stop at nothing to stop me cold."

"What's the scheme?"

"Overpopulation chokes the world to within an inch of its life. Fishing stocks are depleted to near exhaustion; global warming gobbles coastlines, extreme weather batters the planet, and food shortages occur with increasing frequency. We're burning this world down to the ground and no one has a solution. But I do."

"I'm all ears."

"Our population explosion is unsustainable and unstoppable. Attempts to limit breeding show spotty results at best. My way is the motorway to a sustainable future."

"Specifics?"

"Put simply, if you halve the size of human beings, you can double the population without increasing the amount of damage to the planet or using any more resources."

"Halve the size of humans? What do you mean?"

"Literally reducing humans to fifty percent of their present size."

108

"You're sending me up." I couldn't tell if he was joking or off his nut.

"Never been more serious in my life. In fact, I've proven this works brilliantly."

"Why haven't I heard of this?"

"Knowing my research would prove controversial, I've kept everything quite hush-hush. Naturally, the government found out anyway and had me arrested on trumped-up charges. I had connections enough to stop them, at least for now. They won't give up because my solution would initially put a dent in corporate profits. They'd like to frame me and toss me in jail."

"What have you accomplished?"

"Quite a lot, really. On our second generation we've achieved a forty-two percent savings in materials and energy while reducing pollution sixty-two percent. We do this by shrinking people by half. It's homunculus in full flower, enjoying fruitful lives in a pilot city.

"How would I know that you're not some raving nutter haunting train stations to spin wild tales?"

"Happy to show you proof. I'm on my way there now."

This was too good to miss. Given my uncertainty about returning to London, his offer was tempting; it would provide time to delay my decision.

I changed my destination to Cornwall. Freebinder and I scored an empty compartment where I grabbed my favorite window seat. Tricky Dick sat beside me, nodding out as we clickety-clacked past quaint-looking farms and villages. Eventually I spotted a high fence with warning signs and concertina wire. A sign warned off the curious, Energy Research Lab, Entry Restricted. A few miles later we arrived at the station, disembarked, and climbed into Freebinder's slate-grey Micro. We motored along for a few miles before passing through towering gates of steel into a brave new world.

Daylight was softly filtered by a camo-scrim covering the entire town. Absolutely everything was half-scaled to fit little folks who scurried about. Tiny buildings towered over wee electric cars driven by geezers less than a meter tall. They seemed a happy lot from what I could tell, but I soon discovered that being a giant isn't nearly as shinky as it might seem.

"A giant among men," Freebinder read my mind.

"Not sure I like it."

Smiling sympathetically, he introduced me to the honorable Mr. P.T. Bedrock, Esq. The cherubic mayor of Tiny Town was a cheery chap wearing a kilt and smelling of chocolate and cigar smoke. He reached a tiny hand up to shake from down below my belt buckle.

"Welcome sir, to Tiny Town, where little people dare to dream big." His voice was deep in a small way.

"Very nice to meet you." I bent down to shake his tiny paw. Invited to a walking tour, we took to the street. Cute little stores emptied of shoppers who ran outside, craning their necks to see the visiting giant.

WE STAND TALLEST WHEN WE SHRINK TO FIT TOMORROW read a wall projection. I saw others as we walked along: BIG FOLKS = BIG WASTE, and HOMUNCULUS? COME JOIN US!

We finished our tour and rejoined Freebinder, "So, you see, my idea's working out quite well." He smiled with obvious pride.

"How long have you been at this?"

"Finding the first round of couples that would allow me to shrink their offspring took some time. Once I had a first generation to prove my case, things got easier. Of course, the smalls wanted children at their scale.

Don't know your plans, but if you'd like to stay awhile, I can offer work and lodgings. We need a past-sized man to help with high-altitude tasks. I'm getting too old for the physical stuff."

"Past-sized?"

"No offense, I'm a dinosaur, too."

"Where would I stay?"

"I have full-sized quarters for visitors. Doesn't pay much, but there's free room and board."

And so I became the only normal-sized man jack in Tiny Town besides its creator. Dead broke and conflicted about returning to London, I don't care much where I am. If it provides food and a place to lay my head, I'm fine.

23 June

As I lie in bed reading news on MemBrain this
morning, Mayor Bedrock burst in, totally panicked,
"Emergency!" He sputtered. "Rabid beast! Terrorizing
the village! Help us! You've got to do something! Quick
man! Get up!"

I jumped out of bed in tee shirt and boxers. He
handed me a carpenter's hammer and pumped my hand
like a captain sending a soldier off to battle.

I ran to the village square—a total panic scene.
Hysterical little geezers scurried about everywhere.
Bedrock pointed at their wee pub. "Got 'im cornered in
there, but good. 'E's in there! In there!" He held a tiny
pitchfork, the perfect accessory for his khaki jodhpurs
and battered pith helmet topped with a flashing,
miniature red beacon. *Tiny Town Defense Force* was
stenciled across its brim in bright red letters.

"Good job, Bedrock. I'll take it from here," I wanted
to strike straight away, but couldn't fit inside the wee
pub. "Somehow." I said through gritted teeth, "I'll get
him. I'll smoke him out. Or something." I hadn't a clue
'til I thought of Tricky Dick and what a perfect fit for
the job he'd be. It was time he earned his keep.

As I hurried back to the bunkroom to fetch Dick, a
rousing anthem boomed over loudspeakers.

You take what you can get
When you're small as a pet
But we don't sweat
And we don't fret
'Cause we'll win in the end, you bet
When the world comes 'round
To shrinking down
And everyone moves
To Tiny Town

Judging by the panicky citizens running about, it
wasn't reassuring them. I fetched Dick and tried to
explain his mission by loudly repeating simple phrases
while gesturing wildly. He paid rapt attention for a bit
and started to laugh. I stressed the seriousness of the
situation. This struck him as even funnier. Then he got
bored. Finally I motioned to the pub and shouted; "Go!"
in a commanding voice. He looked at me with an

expression that said, "No," so I grabbed his hand and dragged him to the pub as fast as I could. Before he had a chance to resist, I pushed him inside. An awful row started up with much wailing and knocking about. After a short bit, Dick ran outside at full speed with a very pissed-off rat at his tail.

I ran after them until they dashed into a narrow crack between two buildings. Trapped in a dead end, the rodent attempted escape by turning and running directly at me. As it approached at top speed, I hurled the hammer, scoring a lucky shot precisely between its shoulders. It collapsed with a bloody squeal. A thick pool of crimson immediately formed 'round its fat, twitching head as Tiny Town citizens gathered 'round with their anxious faces relaxing to grateful smiles. Several tried to high-five me, but bending down to reach their little palms soon grew tiresome.

Tiny Towners broke out their rousing anthem again to cheer my victory over the rogue rodent.

You take what you can get
When you're small as a pet
But we don't sweat
And we don't fret . . .

Dick didn't forget what he'd found in the pub. While we were distracted with our congratulations, he slipped back inside and got busy with the beer tap. Tired of congratulatory speeches and out of tune caroling, I bid goodbye and left to find him. I didn't have to go far as Dick soon stumbled 'round a corner, knocked me down and climbed on my chest to slobber a wet kiss. Gagging on his hot monkey beer breath, I tossed him off, grabbed his paw and tried to calm him with a walk, but he slipped my grip and ran off on a drunken rampage.

Drunken Dick proved to be a different monkey than the mellow traveling companion I'd gotten used to, more like Godzilla on acid, wreaking much havoc before I could stop him. He'd saved the day and deserved a pint, but I was sad to see my fears about his drinking were justified.

I've learned one thing: a drunken monkey is much less fun than it sounds. I only hope Dick learns a lesson from his upcoming hangover.

24 June

At the crack of dawn, little folks appeared with a marching band outside my window, braying that anthem at the top of their lungs. Is it the only song they know? I stuck my head out the window to quiet them. Mayor Bedrock saw me, held up a hand, and they stopped cold.

Bedrock made a phlegmy, throat-clearing sound amplified by a wee electric megaphone and addressed the crowd, "Ahem . . . I, P.T. Bedrock, as duly elected mayor of Tiny Town, hereby declare today, June 24st, 2048, to be Ignatius Fumbo Day, in honor of his courageous action in saving our community from the attack of a vicious beast. Let the celebration begin!"

Music and singing resumed, louder than ever. There was a knock. A groggy mess in boxers, tee shirt, and stubble, I opened the door on the good mayor who presented me with a parchment scroll that extolled my bravery while noting my keen aim with a carpenter's hammer. I bent down so he could hang a flash-looking medal 'round my neck.

"As Tiny Town's most honoured savior, we invite you to march at the head of our victory parade."

"Appreciate the invitation, but not really dressed for a parade." I slipped on a pair of jeans and a tee shirt.

"Oh, we're quite casual here in Tiny Town, quite casual indeed. Rouse your monkey! We have something for him, too." The mayor held up a smaller version of the clunky gold medallion he'd given me.

"Dick won't be joining us this morning. He's a bit under the weather."

"Berrach!" The sound of a vomiting monkey echoed from the bath, underscoring my point.

"Well then, won't you come along then? The villagers will be terribly disappointed if you don't join us."

I marched through the streets of Tiny Town, a rumpled hero smiling down on scores of mini-citizens leaning out of tiny buildings and waving. The band played an instrumental version of their anthem as a blizzard of tiny ticker tape snowed down below my waist.

Amongst all the gaiety, I felt the loneliness only a giant could know.

25 June

Awoke to a bleary morning after one too many toasts at the testimonial dinner. This hangover is enough to convince me I'm not cut out to be a hero. I sipped water and surfed MemBrain, but found nothing of interest.

Tricky Dick awoke in a mellow mood as I sat on the small porch behind our quarters, gazing at a little tree in the garden and felt like I was floating free in a life with no more substance than specks of dust drifting lazily in summer sunbeams.

Then it hit me why I felt this way. I no longer need this ramble. I don't belong here. My home is with my mates.

"What do you think, Dick? Are you ready to leave?" Dick, the re-hydrating Monkey looked up from his juice box with an expression I took as agreement.

I wanted to explain things to my hosts before I changed my mind, so I walked to Freebinder's cottage where I found him wearing a Sherlock Holmes deerstalker hat and smoking hashish from a white clay pipe. "Yes, yes, my boy. By all means come in, come in, and have a puff of Arabee." He handed me the pipe. I took a drag of spicy resin smoke and copped a coughing fit.

"So," he laughed, "how'd it feel to wake up as a hero this morning?"

"Well, besides a blinding headache from my hangover, not so bad."

He laughed again, reached into a brandy glass filled with tiny chocolates the size of blue berries, grabbed a handful and offered them to me. When I declined, he stuffed them in his mouth and rolled his eyes back, smacking his lips with great relish.

"Sorry to burst in on you like this, but I'm thinking I'd best rejoin my mates in the band. I'll be leaving for London today."

Bedrock stopped chewing immediately, stashed a lump of chocolate in his chubby cheek and stared at me wide-eyed.

"You're leaving Tiny Town? Really? But we've planned a royal cavalcade for you this very night. There'll be pageantry. Pageantry, I tell you! And there's our gala Thank You Breakfast tomorrow. The citizens will be crushed. Isn't there some way you could delay this until tomorrow evening? It would mean the world to us here in Tiny Town if we could give you a proper send-off."

I just want to leave, I thought. I want to go now. But for some reason, I couldn't say no to a three-foot tall chocoholic Caesar. I mumbled with what little sincerity I could muster, "Oh, okay sure. I guess."

I left a note expressing my regrets and split when no one was looking. And there I was, on the road again with my pal Tricky Dick. I thought I'd hitch a ride to the station and cadge fare from a sympathetic traveller, but ended up stalking a busted-up lane clogged with grannies in pods and kids on trikes dodging potholes. Not a good day for hitching. They had no interest in stopping. They just stared at us with what vague curiosity. Didn't seem like Dick enjoyed the walk, but he held my hand and ambled along like a real trooper.

The sun was setting, so I found some brush and using some full-sized blankets I nicked at Tiny Town, made a quick bed off the roadside. Soon enough, me and my monkey were set for the night on a cosy cushion of leaves.

26 – 31 June

No luck hitching a ride. We trudged on with little of interest to report. Two brief rides were all we managed over five days. We slept in bushes, a trackside shack, and the porch of an abandoned house. Dick shows increasing signs of turning cranky and so do I.

1 July

THE HIVE WELCOMES
OUR GODS' RETURN

Crude letters glittered on a homemade sign hung by the entrance to a neglected looking, overgrown park dotted with colourful tents. Nasty-looking, spiky weeds poked through the broken pavement of what had once been a car park. Rusting cars sinking into the earth on flattened tires and busted springs had been re-purposed as living quarters.

"Is this a cult?" I asked a thin bird with a heart-shaped face, jet-black hair with fringe halfway covering her eyes. She stood by a faded orange tent in jodhpurs, suede Chelsea boots, a pearl-snap western shirt, and a ten-gallon hat like a silent movie cowboy.

"Sort of. They believe aliens will drop in for a visit once they've prepared things properly. They're looking for a location to build a landing strip."

"Aren't you with them?"

"I'm not with them in spirit, just here as a companion to me mum. She hopes the aliens will arrive in time to cure her cancer. She's off in their medical tent now."

"Mind if I crash here?" I was too knackered for small talk.

She smiled yes, "What brings you here?"

"Rambling about. Could use a kip."

"Honest bugger." She snapped her gum like a punctuation mark.

"Tired bugger, actually."

Set my pack on the ground and sat on a three-legged canvas campstool. One of its aluminum legs slowly sunk into the soft earth, but being too tired to care, I rode it all the way down like a stone-faced Keaton 'til it tipped me over in a slow-motion slapstick scene. She laughed explosively and offered a hand to help me up.

"I'm Emma, Where are you off to next?"

"Ignatius Fumbo." We shook. "Home. I am going home."

"And that would be . . .?"

"London. Have some mates waiting for me."

Emma's sparkling hazel eyes gleamed seductively from under the brim of her hat as she scanned me like a cat.

Leading me into her tent and without a word said, Emma took me and shook me. She shook me cold. Thank you, road gods. Thank you very much.

Afterwards, we lay there quietly for a while, kissing sweetly before Emma whispered, "It's all holograms, innit?"

Not this again, I thought. What's on with everyone obsessing over sub-atomic physics?

"All is energy. It gives a convincing imitation of solidity, but reality is, there's more space than solid in things—and in us. Everything's just collections of tiny buzzing particles whirling about, too fast to question and it's all connected."

"Sounds familiar." I kissed Emma's cheek again. She smiled and kissed me back.

We walked a forest path as quiet as a temple with our steps cushioned by a thick carpet of pine needles. The campground's cobbled-together shower shack was a welcome sight. I lathered up with liquid peppermint soap Emma supplied. Walking back to her tent through the cool forest, I felt clean as a sunbeam.

"You can rest here," she pointed to her tent, "but first I'll bring tea. Then I'm off to visit mum."

She returned and with a pot of steaming hot, earthy-smelling tea. "Special tea," she smiled.

Emma closed the tent flap as she left. I took my boots off and lay down on a folding cot. Off in the distance, a spooky-sounding flute played primal earth music as I watched tree shadows play on tent walls. After sipping the tea to its last drop, I dozed off.

An hour later, I was jolted awake by the hooting of some animal.

Unrolling MemBrain, I tapped this out:
It's all a hologram
That's what she said
She said
Everything's a ghost
She said, even us two
And then she took me

And she shook me
She shook me cold
She said listen, you
Everything's a ghost
She said, even we two
That's what she said
And then she took me
And she shook me
She shook me cold

Looking excited, Emma stuck her head in the tent, "Merge in fifteen minutes!"

"Merge?"

"They gather in the forest. Omar channels some alien shite and gives everyone a brain buzz."

"Alien shite?"

"He claims to channel alien mental energy to his audience."

"Nutty."

"It's actually a brilliant mind fuck—you should try it once."

"Why don't you?"

"I did, but stopped while I still could. It's addictive and I'm not so keen on this scene to start."

Following Emma's directions, I trod silently through a spooky forest where ancient trees formed a cooling canopy of darkness. Off in the distance, others trudged along going the same way. Mangy-looking deer with blackened coats and dull expressions grazed here and there. Eventually our paths merged until we flowed together like a river of humanity.

We came to a clearing where an unpainted wooden stage glowed eerily in electric blue twilight. A high cheek-boned geezer with multi-coloured mirrors on his hobnail boots stood erect behind a glass lectern. Meter tall illuminated letters a served as backdrop:

IF YOU'VE DONE NOTHING WRONG
YOU HAVE NOTHING TO FEAR

Our hawk-eyed commander hushed us with a finger to his lips and pointed at an empty, twilight blue sky. I stared upwards too long and my neck cramped. Finally, a glowing white disc appeared out of nowhere, so bright I couldn't catch an outline or judge its size. A low hum of alternating notes ramped up strong enough to rattle my fillings. I felt all resistance melt as a strangely pleasant, electric buzz swept over me. Suddenly, I wasn't me. I was everybody, joining in to form a kind of meat mainframe.

I had no idea how much time had passed when suddenly, the hum stopped cold. The disc brightened for a second, popped out, and vanished. My buzz quickly faded leaving me standing in a darkened forest with an odd lot of geezers smiling at each other with rapturous, empty-headed gazes. I didn't join them. I was cold and hungry. My feet were damp. I had a crick in my neck and a crack in my lip.

I left the others beaming with their frozen grins to make my way back to Emma's tent where I found her lying on a cot, watching a vid on MemBrain, "Enjoy your merge?" she asked.

"I did. It was strangely pleasurable."

"Don't make it a habit."

"Why's that?"

"I'm sure it felt fantastic, but it's actually a hive-mind synchronization device. A few more sessions and you'll become a zombie goofball like the rest of this lot."

I had a mild headache, but felt an urge to merge again as soon as possible, while suspecting that Emma hadn't exaggerated its danger.

12 July

Sorry I've neglected you, Dear Diary. This lovely idyll with Emma has left lackadaisical and uninspired to write. But I've made a decision. I'll rejoin my comrades and see things through, come what may.

When I opened MemBrain to email Beddy and Gearly the news, an alert came on; I'd subscribed to mentions of the Blow Goes.

Clicking on the *New Music Express* link, a headline struck a hammer blow,

BLOW GOES TO REPLACE
MISSING KEYBOARDIST.

What the bloody hell?

I read on:

*Blow Goes' manager Major Boyle has announced
auditions to replace their missing keyboardist. "Ignatius
Fumbo's absence has brought the band's momentum to
a screeching halt. We can't afford to wait while the
boys' opportunities dry up. With great regret, The Blow
Goes are moving on to find a new member."*

What a cunt that Major Boyle has turned out. Never
dreamed he'd pull a stunt like this without even a final
contact. Have I muffed my only shot at rock and roll
stardom?

"Read this, Emma. I can't fucking believe it." She
put down her knitting, read intently, and looked up with
a quizzical expression, "What's this got to do with
you?"

"I'm the missing member—the one they're
replacing."

"Really? You were in The Blow Goes?"

"Not were, I *am* in The Blow Goes."

"Sorry, but that looks doubtful now."

"Gotta do something fast."

I found a photo of me and the boys online and
showed it to her.

"Amazing. Why, in the name of rock 'n roll did you
leave?"

"Wasn't playing up to the others' level and didn't
want to hold them back."

"Wouldn't that be their worry?"

"Suppose so. Anyway, I've decided to rejoin them,
but it looks like I've royally fucked myself out of that
opportunity."

"Not necessarily."

"Why's that?"

"According to this, they haven't actually hired
anyone, have they?"

"Who knows? The article's three days old."

I was well and truly freaked; like that sinking feeling
you get when you lose your girl. Plan of action needed
fast or I'm a dead duck.

Needing to stop obsessing and let my subconscious
do the sorting, I visited a pub with Emma and got
royally pissed. Sitting in an oaken booth, she copped to
the scene with her mum, "I can't be there for you now,

Fumbs. Mum has taken a turn. They're only giving her a few more weeks to live. I'll be spending all my spare time with her."

I held her hands across the table top, "Sad news. So sorry to hear. Probably best for all that I move along now."

13 July
Woke up fucked up with a hangover supreme. Good job. Now I'm both sick and forsaken. I borrowed Emma's MemBrain to fire off texts to Bedford, Gearly, and Boyle: *Sorry for the delay, but I'm on my way to rejoin the band, finally and forever. Please don't do anything hasty. Just need to make my way to a train station and I'll be there a.s.a.p.* I hit "send" and got an onscreen message: *SERVICE NOT AVAILABLE.*

"Fuck!" I was in no mood.

"Having a problem?" Emma strummed her ukulele, humming softly with Tricky Dick at her feet, listening with rapt attention.

"Says: Service not available."

"Happens a lot here. Sometimes stays off for days."

"How far is the nearest train station?"

"It's a ways actually, same direction you were headed. Will you be leaving us?"

"I've no choice. I'll have to beg, borrow or steal the fare to London; my future hangs on it."

"I've a few spare creds I can transfer to your account."

"I'll pay you back double."

She laughed. "Don't be silly, glad to help."

Emma proved to be a true angel when I needed one most. Now all I have to do is make my way to the station and hop a coach to London. I'll message the boys once I learn my arrival time.

After we said sad goodbyes, I struck out in the early afternoon. Strong feelings weighted heavy between us, knowing we might never see each other again.

It was a fine weather for hitching a ride, but fixedly staring at screens as their little pods drove along, motorists didn't seem to agree. Apparently, a roadside wanderer was easy to ignore, even one with a monkey on his back. I was grateful that Tricky Dick bore things with his usual stoicism. Just as I was thinking I should have scrawled a sign to flash, a sketchy-looking fellow in a battered Eggo Supreme pulled over. I ran up to meet Skitch, a skinny, unshaven reed of a man with doubly bagged, red-rimmed eyes. Was he a lonely allergy sufferer or into something more sinister? I was in no position to judge, so I eagerly clambered into the seat behind him and set Tricky Dick on my lap. Skitch had on music that sounded like monks chanting as they banged on sheet metal.

Got him chatting, but that was a mistake. Once Skitch started, there was no stopping the man. I drifted in and out of attention as he nattered on about aliens, dairy-free lifestyles, and do-it-yourself trike maintenance. After an hour of this, the sound of dreary monks banging on sheet metal seemed preferable. But then he said something that got my attention; "You unlock the door of reality with the key of imagination, that's what I think."

"What door is that," I asked.

"The door to a loving universe that provides all you need, when you need it, without effort."

"How's that work?"

"If you're grateful for what you have and feel good, I mean, really good, and conjure up the emotion you'll feel when you get what you seek, you'll attract things without effort. The more you feel it's real, the realer it'll be. The universe is as we conceive it. It's about being in tune and letting things flow towards you, see?"

"That's similar to what I learned in a self-help course I recently took."

Once Skitch ran out his string of chat, we cruised along in silence, watching a programme about Mexican pyramids. I spoke during a break, "I just hope things slow down long enough for me to reclaim my job before I'm sacked."

"What job is that?"

"I was playing keyboards in a band. Wasn't technically up to the others' level so I took off to sort things. But I've stayed away too long and they're replacing me."

"Sorry to hear."

"Serves me right. I'm running back to save my job."

"What band?"

"The Blow Goes."

"Really? The Blow Goes spin my plates. Much respect." Skitch high-fived me, took a few pulls from a flask and offered me some. I took a sip of what tasted like high-octane tequila. He leaned back, nodded out, and began to snore loudly with his head resting against the trike's Perspex canopy causing an annoying rattle right next to my ear. This added to the barely-in-control feeling of a self-guided plastic pod hurtling along at 80 miles per hour. I hugged my monkey tight as the landscape blurred past.

Checking schedules on Skitch's screen, I was disappointed to learn there won't be a train to London 'til noon.

Unfortunately, Skitch wasn't going all the way to the station. He let me off in the darkness at the edge of town. It was late, spookily quiet, and still. Not a single pod around for hitching a ride.

Our trip to the station could wait for morning. I put Dick down, handed him his water bottle and sat on the curb to rummage through my backpack for the granola bars Emma had made for us. I washed two down with hearty gulps of coconut juice. They hit the spot. Dick liked his, too.

Looking for a spot to grab a kip, I spied an abandoned-looking storefront. Stepping over crumpled up newspapers obstructing the entrance, I pulled open a dingy, enameled yellow steel door. It creaked open into a darkened chamber where strange equipment glowed an intense electric blue. There was a smell like electricity gone wrong. Silhouetted in smoky glare, a tall, gangly figure darted about.

"Don't just stand there like a dipshit!" A harsh voice echoed across the cavernous cement room, startling Dick. He jumped into my arms. The figure beckoned us forward.

I walked across a dusty cement floor watching the strange figure hunching over some kind of console. Dick looked up at me with a skeptical expression as we approached to crackling electric sounds and multi-coloured flying sparks. I was surprised to see our host was a lady. She wore a black lab coat, goggles and elbow length gloves. Her raven black hair was tied up in an elaborate topknot, adding greatly to her already towering height, further enhanced by sky-high platform boots. She slammed a heavy metal door on a thick-walled chamber before I could see what was inside.

"What's your business?" She croaked.

"No business at all. Just looking for a spot to grab a kip."

"Ha!" She croaked a rusty, artificial-sounding laugh. "Well, you won't get any sleep around here, I'll be working all night. What's on with that monkey?"

"Inherited him when his owner was killed in a motor crash."

"I could use a primate subject. Want to sell him?"

"Sorry, no. We're mates."

"Well, you're wasting my time. If you'd be so kind as to find another bedroom, I'll get back to work."

"What kind of work is this?"

"Prying open a lock to peek inside the chest."

"What chest is that?"

"The intersection of energy, frequency, and vibration. Cracking the sublime power that moves galaxies, an understanding of gravity, time, and space."

"Oh, that. Shouldn't take you all night."

"Ha!" She laughed, just as unconvincingly as before. I grabbed Dick's hand and turned to walk away.

"Wait," she called out.

"What is it?"

"I'd enjoy some company, actually. There's a motor caravan out back with an extra bunk and room for a monkey."

I was leery of her, but exhaustion won out.

"Yes. We're quite knackered. Thanks."

She extended her hand, "I'm Olive."

"Ignatius Fumbo."

"It's out in the alley. Blankets are in the cupboard; eat, drink what you like."

Dick and I stretched out in the cosy, wood-lined motor-caravan that smelled of ripe bananas. I found a bunch in a cupboard and gave Dick three. Made myself a cuppa tea with biscuits. Dick curled up at the lower end of the bed. I threw on a tartan blanket and conked out.

14 July

I awoke to metallic screams from a starter motor that sounded like it hadn't been oiled since the queen died.

"Start, you rotter! Start now or I'll pack you in."

The engine coughed to life. Olive jammed that bitch into first gear and we jerked forward, bouncing down a bombed-out alley like a crazy amusement park ride.

I crept up behind Olive and asked her flat, "What's on?"

"Miscalculation in my computation. The pile could blow. If it doesn't we'll be clear in twenty-four hours. Must split 'til then."

"And if it blows?"

"You don't wanna know. There's nothing anyone can do to stop it now. No one's in any danger, but it could leave a very deep hole."

"Where are we headed?"

"London. Got hook-ups."

"Excellent, I'm headed that way too."

Even a loser gets lucky sometimes.

Unfortunately, a mechanical breakdown forced us to wait for spares. The motor caravan sat stilled, as sad and useless as a beached whale.

16 July

The spares showed up late yesterday. Olive said she'd install them in the morning and we'd be on our way. Hurray to that.

Drunk on brandy last night, Olive said she'd reveal what she was really working on if I swore confidentiality. I eagerly agreed to sign her non-disclosure agreement.

"I'm developing a virtual other peoples' reality viewer," she blurted. "A helmet with goggles that will enable the wearer to see the world through another's eyes — an epic, world-changing breakthrough in human consciousness. Swap brains and settle arguments, negotiate peace treaties, and so on. The possibilities are limitless."

"Really?"

"Really."

"How's it work?"

"It fucks with the space/time continuum,"
was all she said. I understood her paranoia—hard to tell what might offend the authorities these days.

Before Olive got busy with a spanner under the bonnet, she handed me a fistful of cred coins and sent me off to fetch groceries. I grabbed my pack and set out, leaving Tricky Dick behind to rest in the motor caravan.

A few miles down the road, I found a corner mini-market surprisingly well stocked—at least well enough to supply crackers, tinned soup, bangers, juice, yogurt, cheddar, apples, and some bananas for Dick. Mission accomplished, I strolled back to the car park where I received an immediate shock—Olive's motor caravan was gone, leaving a rather large hole in what had been my reality. Assuming she'd finished the repair and was off for quick road test, I sat under a nearby tree to enjoy an apple and a bite of cheddar while I texted her.

No reply was forthcoming.

I waited and texted again as I began to wonder if the repair might have failed and left Olive stranded. But why wasn't she answering texts? Was something sinister going on? I texted the same message for the third time: *Where are you? Waiting here at the car park. Please check in.*

Hours passed with no answer. My hope dimmed with the setting sun. Left with time to think, I recalled Olive asking about buying Tricky Dick for use as a test subject. It was odd, the way she initially sent me off, then suddenly changed her mind and let me stay in her caravan. Had she planned this all along, seizing an opportunity to be rid of me and kidnap Dick for some evil experiment? I always felt suspicious, like she might have something up her sleeve.

Then I remembered Dick's GPS tracer embed. Excitedly, I unrolled MemBrain, found the app, entered his name and password, and watched a wee ball spin for what seemed an eternity before it finally froze as a bold

notice flashed onscreen, SERVICE NOT AVAILABLE.
This was not optimum timing. I felt like throwing that
MemBrain across the car park, but had to stay cool and
think things through. I thought of alerting the police, but
showing up in their database as an escaped mental
patient raving about a kidnapped monkey might not play
out well.

In the meantime, I will lose my job if I don't get my
ass back to London soon, as in now.

Bloody hell.

Thought I should stay at the car park; if Dick
escaped he might find his way back. But that seemed a
bad choice compared to the pressing need to find a
working Wi-Fi cell and search via GPS.

The sun was setting when I started off, hoping to
find Olive tinkering under the caravan's bonnet
somewhere along the motorway or, failing that, at least
cop a working cell for MemBrain. As I trudged along
feeling anxious as hell, I became more and more
convinced that this wasn't about a post-repair
breakdown, but a straight ahead case of monkey-
napping—and if that's true, I've got to find Dick before
Olive has time to conduct some fiendish experiment.

Missing Dick terribly, I hitched along a dismal,
nearly empty motorway. The paltry few passing pods
took little notice of my extended thumb as they buzzed
past with their passengers staring at screens. It came as
no surprise that they didn't react like those who'd seen
Dick strapped to my back. With each sorry step, my
anxiety level rose. Where in God's name could she be?

Desperate for a working cell, I kept checking
reception. After a couple hours, eureka! I scored a fat
four bars reception, found a spot to sit, and entered
Dick's info into the finder app. It took a few minutes
before spotting him along the motorway to London—the
same route we'd traveled prior to the breakdown.
Making good time, Olive was miles ahead and traveling
fast. Even if I were to catch a ride, how could I possibly
catch her?

As I sat there thinking, a text from Boyle popped up,
*Where in God's name are you? I've scheduled a press
conference to announce your replacement on eighteen*

July. If you're not here, I'm sorry, but you're out of the band. We've got a great candidate on deck. I can't sacrifice the others' future waiting around for you to show up.

I wanted to write back, *Thank you so very much, my dear Mister Boyle. Love you too, mate—and, by the way, your timing is impeccable,* but thought better of it. Instead I wrote: *On my way, please hold on. Arriving soon.*

Trudging along with thumb out and head down, I felt my last crumbs of hope slip away. What's next? I've lost my monkey and I'm about to lose my band.

I felt desperate enough to think of praying for the first time in my life. Anybody up there interested in helping a desperate stranger? At my wit's end and having nothing to lose, I swallowed my pride and whispered a solemn prayer for Dick's salvation.

Then I recalled that Olive refused to drive at night. This might provide a lucky break, allowing time to catch up if I can score a ride from this lot of tossers.

Feeling dejected, I sat with my thumb out. After half an hour, a sleek silver pod with rude writing scrawled down its sides slowed to take a look at me. As they stopped, I saw the lipstick scrawl referred to recent nuptials. So excited to cop a ride, I nearly jumped into their four-seater pod.

Ian and Sylvia were honeymooners out for fun. They asked for my story as soon as I'd squeezed into their backseat.

"I'm an escapee from a mental facility, currently searching for a monkey that was nicked by a mad scientist for an evil experiment."

"Funny bit, but really," Sylvia looked concerned, "what are you about?"

"Know it sounds utterly barmy, but it's stone cold fact. I've located her caravan via GPS finder. She's some miles up ahead."

Sylvia looked incredulous, "You're actually serious? Why would anyone steal your monkey?"

"Said she wants to use him as a test subject in some experiment."

"Oh dear," Sylvia looked worried, "Scary. Why did you escape a mental facility?"

"A long story, but actually, it was a halfway house. I'm considered cured, as far as that goes."

"Our destination is past that GPS point, maybe you'll get lucky." Ian said.

"Great to hear, thanks."

"Is she dangerous?"

"Dunno, really. She's a mystery wrapped in an enigma. I'll have to take my chances."

Riding along in silence as darkness fell. Ian put on some ambient chill. We had miles to go, no problem if Olive had really stopped for the night.

After writing this, I felt sleepy—the stress had caught up with me. Dozed off and dreamed of picnicking at Hyde Park with Jelly and Dick. Half an hour later, I awoke and checked my super combi watch Sky View Finder app. Great news, Olive's caravan hadn't budged. We were closing in fast.

Sky View Finder showed her parked beneath an overpass. Surprise attacks work best. I should enter the caravan through its roof hatch.

Anxious, I checked my watch every few minutes, causing the miles to crawl by. Then suddenly, we were just a few miles out, homing in fast. She hadn't moved an inch.

"Closing in, Ignatius. We should formulate a plan." Ian seemed keen to help. Had my prayer been answered?

"I was thinking of entering the caravan through its roof hatch to surprise her, grab Dick, and beat a hasty retreat. But how to do that is the question."

"Does the word 'rappel' mean anything to you?" Ian smiled.

I wondered what he was on about.

"Must really be your lucky day, 'cause I'm actually a rock climber, and a good one, if I say so myself. I travel equipped."

I was surprised that Ian would be so insensitive as to send me up at this time. "Not joking?"

"Dead serious, mate."

Apparently good luck is so unpredictable it can even happen to me.

"Oh boys, what jolly good adventure!" Sylvia glowed with excitement.

Ian gestured toward his screen; "Map shows a cut-off a mile past her location. I say we pop off the motorway there and double back on the access road to the overpass. Once there, I'll rig you up for a little drop-in party."

"Sounds perfect." As we motored past, the Caravan looked sweetly innocent with its lights aglow. I could only wonder what horrors lurked within.

Doubling back, we parked on the shoulder of the overpass where Ian anchored a line to the railing and the other end to my harness, explaining things as he rigged me up.

Gently lowering me onto the caravan's roof, Ian watched as I landed softly, tread quietly to the hatch and yanked it with all my might. To my shock, it was unfastened and popped open with a loud squeak.

And there I was, staring directly into Olive's outraged face, both of us frozen in shock. I tried to lower myself inside before she could make a move, but she'd armoured up with a cast iron fry pan and used it to batter my legs. I dodged her blows by thrashing about like I was treading water. A lucky kick knocked her back and I dropped inside. She came at me, still batting away like a maniac while Dick jumped up and down in a crude-looking corner cage; shadow boxing as if encouraging me.

Olive's willowy frame made a poor match for a scrapper like me. Dodging her blows, I fell to the floor, grabbed her ankles, and pulled her down with a mighty thud. Hopping on top, I pinned her in classic wrestling style. She screeched at top volume, "Help! Rape! Help! Attack! I'm being Attacked. Help!"

I held a hand over Olive's mouth as she furiously thrashed about. "Consider yourself lucky I'm not bashing your fool head in and don't move a muscle or I'll give you something to holler about."

After I jumped up and freed Dick from his cage, Olive approached from behind. I turned just in time to see her, grabbed her arm with a ju-jitsu move and twisted it around behind her back, forcing her to drop the weapon. I held her arm tightly so she couldn't move without pain, but she continued to struggle like a mad woman, so I picked up the pan and bashed her on the noggin. That seemed to temper Olive's more aggressive tendencies, leaving her slumping, propped up against a wall. I could almost make out cartoon stars circling 'round her head.

I grabbed Dick and clambered out the caravan's door, dragging rope and rigging behind. It was a short climb up to the access road where Ian and Sylvia waited.

"Great work, Ignatius. This must be the famous Tricky Dick." Smiling big, Ian and Sylvia shook hands with my favourite monkey.

"Thanks. Got it done, if not without a bit of a row. I've a feeling Olive will not soon forget this caper."

As we stood there congratulating ourselves, a dark figure approached from below. It was Olive, running at full gallop, still waving that fry pan. Just as before, I dove for her legs, toppled her onto the gravel and straddled her wrestler-style.

Ian tied her up with ropes and we carried Olive back down to her motor caravan where we laid her gently on the floor.

"We'll leave you alone to give you time to think on what you've done,"

Dick was hyped and jumpy, but happy to see me. I gave him a water bottle he sucked like he was dying of thirst.

Another text came through from Boyle, *Having not received positive confirmation regarding your timely return to London, we are forced to proceed with a press conference announcing our new hire on keyboards, 18 July.* \

"We?" Who the bloody hell is "we?" Hate to think Bedford and Gearly are in on this plot. Didn't feel like honouring Boyle with a reply, but thought it best to stay on the safe side.

I'll explain later, but there's been a hold up. On my way to London now. Please cancel press conference.

All too soon, Ian and Sylvia arrived at their exit. "Sorry, but we have to drop you off; our honeymoon cottage lies down the road. You've plenty of time to make it to London by your deadline. Best of luck."

We traded emails and they were off, leaving Dick and I in a familiar roadside situation. Unfortunately, our crummy hitching luck was back on. There was no traffic to speak of, so we stood, and sat, and stood again.

After fretting there for a couple hours, the headlights of a pod approached. As it slowed, I jumped up and high-fived Dick. Then I saw it was a police pod.

A brain-etchingly bright light shone in our faces as I stood up in the full confidence of an innocent man, no crime having been committed other than fleeing the halfway. They're probably just checking to make sure I'm not some roadside criminal type.

"Drop to the ground! Spread your arms and legs!"

What the bloody hell? She spoke with exclamation points, so I knew better than to disobey.

"Let's see your ID."

I pulled it out and handed it over, then dropped to their commanded position.

"I see. . . just as we thought. Cuff 'im, Nigel."

Nigel handcuffed my arms behind my back and pulled me up.

"If you don't mind my asking, what's this all about?"

"Assault complaint and a theft report."

"Assault? Theft? What?"

"Suppose you're going to claim that monkey as your very own traveling companion, then?"

Damn that Olive. Damn her to an eternal hell of fried circuits and rusty synapses.

They hauled me to the station, fingerprinted me, stuck me in a dodgy cell with a drippy toilet, and slammed a heavy iron door shut. But I'd caught a lucky break. They didn't know what to do with Dick, so they stuck him in here with me.

As we sat on the edge of the cot, Dick looked up with a quizzical, "What now?" expression. I couldn't help it; I had to laugh at our situation. A much-needed relief, but once started, I couldn't stop; I got hysterical and Dick joined in, too. Right in the middle of our

giggle fit, two cops stopped by. One held a MemBrain
and stood there looking at me queerly.

"Happy to see you're having such a good time here,
Mister Fumbo. My, my, your charges are piling up
nicely. Databank says you're an escaped mental patient.
Let's see: escape from a halfway house, theft, assault,
animal abuse—all this could put you away for a very
long rest, indeed."

"I doubt you'll believe me, but truth is, Dick here is
actually *my* monkey, and that mad Olive lady nicked
him. When I went to retrieve him, she attacked me. So,
if it's not too much bother, could you tell me how long
might it take to clear this matter up so we can be on our
way? I've an important meeting in London, day after
tomorrow."

"Oh, you have an important meeting, do you? And
on the day after tomorrow, too! Why didn't you say
something? Sorry if we've held you up, sir, so very
sorry, indeed. This has all been most inconsiderate of us.
Maybe we ought to just let you go now and forget the
whole thing?" Both cops burst out in hysterical laughter
that carried on far too long. I stared at the floor waiting
for them to stop, but they kept it up, slapping each other
on their backs and giggling 'til tears rolled down their
chubby pink cheeks.

After they finally left, and, though knackered from a
trying day, I wrote this to you, Dear Diary. Then I
nodded out with Dick cuddled against my back.

17 July

Something tugged at my shirt, waking me in the
middle of the night. It was Dick, hopping up and down,
pulling on my arm. I got up and padded across the
concrete floor in stocking feet. Standing at the iron door
to my cell, I swear Dick was smiling as he slipped
between the bars and got busy picking the lock with the
skill of a surgeon. I pulled the door open. The trickster
had done it again; just like when he'd picked the lock in
that dodgy seaman's hotel.

I looked out at the corridor; a short hallway led to
what looked like an exit door. Freedom was so very
close. Holding Dick's hand, we tiptoed down the

hallway. Was the door wired with an alarm? I didn't see any option but to go for it. So I went for it.

I picked up Dick and BAM! Threw that door open and sprinted across the car park, running for our lives. An alarm sounded, louder than bombs.

I pumped with all I had 'til I hit a pothole and stumbled. Struggling like a pratfall clown, I tried desperately to stay on my feet, so I wouldn't fall and injure Tricky Dick.

The jailhouse door opened, spilling light into the deep black night. Nigel the chubby cop flashed a torch across the car park. Barefoot in pygamas, with a stocking cap pulled low enough to nearly cover his beady eyes, he didn't look especially keen on a chase. I crept behind a hedge, ducking low as he ambled out swinging his torch and cursing like a madman.

Crouching low and crab walking as fast as I could, I saw lights on at a nearby cottage and made my way there at top speed. Creeping 'round its perimeter to suss the scene, I had little luck; the drapes were pulled down tight. Then I tripped over a garden rake. Attempting to spare Dick from injury, I tossed him at a nearby bush as I fell. He landed softly, but I didn't share his luck and slammed into a wooden cellar door with a loud crash, gashing my forehead. As I rose, a door opened and a skinny old bearded geezer peered into the dark, holding a torch in one hand and a meat cleaver in the other.

"Who's there?"

"Ignatius here. Ignatius Fumbo." I wiped off blood trickling into my eyes.

"Mind telling me what you're doing creeping 'round here in the middle of the night?"

Dick ambled over to join me.

"We're looking. . . looking for a friend, yes, that's it, we're looking for a friend."

"Really now. Are your friends vampires haunting the night?"

"No, no. You misunderstand; we're actually looking to make a new friend. Yes, that's it! We're looking to make a new friend."

He laughed out loud. "Full credit for originality, but surely you could find a better time and place for that."

He switched off the torch and put the cleaver down. "Got to be careful. There's a jailhouse nearby and our local bobbies are comically inept."

"Of course. I understand. Actually we're just a couple lost travelers. Sorry to disturb you. We'll be on our way." Blood still dripped into my eyes; I wiped them with the back of my sleeve.

"You've a rather nasty scrape there. Pop inside and we'll clean it up."

"Terribly kind of you. Thanks."

We stepped inside his cosy, book-lined cottage. "I'm Hoffman," he said.

I stuck out my hand for a shake, but seeing it was all bloody, we simultaneously shook our heads as if to say no.

"Fumbo, Ignatius Fumbo. Guess I mentioned that."

"And who'd this, then?"

"This here's my boon companion, Tricky Dick."

Hearing his name, Dick jumped into my arms.

Hoffman took me into the bath where he deftly cleansed my wound and applied a stinging astringent.

"Sorry, fresh out of bandages, but at least it's clean."

"That's perfectly fine. Thanks a million."

"Come, have a sit, I'll put a kettle on."

I held a cloth on my forehead to staunch the bleeding as we sat to enjoy our tea.

"My guess is, hardened criminals don't often travel with pets. If it wasn't for that, I'd have pegged you as an escapee straight away."

"Your kindness compels a confession. Actually, I did escape your local authorities. But, please hear me out before you turn me in."

"Everyone has a story and no one's guilty."

"No doubt." I rolled out our tale with Dick sitting on my lap, listening as if it was news to him, too.

"Right then, just to recap: you're an escaped mental patient fleeing jail on an assault charge because you attacked a mad scientist who nicked your monkey for a fiendish experiment and if you can't get to London tomorrow, you'll be sacked from a hot new band that stars the world's greatest drummer. Is that about it?"

"Quite."

"Sounds daft enough to be true, but let's verify." Hoffman popped out a MemBrain and searched The Blow Goes. Links filled pages.

"So, at least we know that bit's true. Once you're back with the band, you'll get massive publicity and it won't be any bother for authorities to look you up. Of course, you can't mention me. They'd book me for aiding flight."

"Agreed, good point. Now, if I might just ask one last favor—we could really use a lift to the nearest station."

"Sod that. Taking the train's daft. That's the first place they'll look. With your hot escapee status and facial recognition CCTVs everywhere, you wouldn't last five minutes."

"Guess I've got things to learn if I'm going to make a career of criminality. Unfortunately, hitching's been spotty; not to mention that motorway cops will be on the lookout, too."

"Seems it's up to me, then?" Hoffman said. Swear I saw a twinkle in his eye.

"I'll guarantee you backstage passes for life."

He laughed. "My pop concert days are well over, but what the hell? I'm long overdue for a visit to London. We best start before everyone's awake and looking for you."

"You rock hard. Thanks a million times."

Hoffman gave Dick a currant bun and banana to munch on while we enjoyed tea and biscuits.

He fired up his Electron 500 and just like that, I was off to rock the world with a mighty little band called The Blow Goes. Got chills thinking on it as we zipped down a pitch black, empty motorway.

Hoffman switched on a screen. Dick fell asleep in my lap as autopilot guided us onto the Motorway. We watched *Cartoon Newz* followed by the weather report, *Clown Time Is Over*.

Having no idea exactly where in London the band might be, I texted Bedford and Gearly. It worked; I had service. Today's miracle momentum appears unstoppable.

18 July

Being back in London gave me a wild buzz.
Hoffman dropped me at the address of a rehearsal space
in Earl's Court that Gearly had texted.

Massive hugs all around. So good to see my mates
again—we were fit to bursting. Even stone-faced
Bedford Vann couldn't wipe off a grin. As we toasted
with sparkling cider, our gear sat waiting like we'd left it
yesterday. They'd framed my amp with a horse collar of
flowers spelling out *Evermore*.

Bedford rang Boyle and told him to call off the
presser announcing my replacement.

Gearly hipped me to the fact that Boyle's released
two songs he'd cobbled together from our jams. He
showed me the charts. Our downloads are on the
upswing. Our streams overflow their banks.

Beddy had a new plan; "Gearly and I feel things
might work better if you switch to bass and lock in on
my rhythms. Losing the programmed bass lines will free
up our groove."

Brilliant.

Gearly re-programmed my keytar as a bass, struck
the opening chord of Bedlam Bay on a hollow-body
twelve string, Beddy hit the tom-toms and we were off.

I darted about like a sandpiper on the shore hunting a
groove, but soon enough, found a lock on Beddy's rock
steady beat. And once we'd synched, we dug that groove
all night long.

20 July

Was it always supposed to be this easy?

Synching my bass lines with Beddy's rock steady
beats works amazingly well and that means I'm pulling
my weight at last. We jammed favourites old and new
'til we nearly dropped. Best bit was when I came up
with a loping bass line for *The Amazing Vet* that,
according to Gearly, "brought it to a new level".

25 July

"Telepathic." Gearly yelped at the wind-out of *A
Brine Man For The Bounty*, a medium tempo rocker
about how it feels pouring salt on your own wounds.

We laid down parts for a new instrumental that Gearly calls *Atmospherical Empirical*, a trippy sail on electric sitar moonbeams that ends up a moody Moogy splashdown into an ocean of tears.

We popped out a funky dance jam, *Four Surprising Reasons to Own Gold*, and worked on another instrumental, *Beware The Robo Mind Control*, titled after a phrase that Gearly whispered at the fade. He's our perfect front man and a crack producer, too.

At the epicenter of crystal blue persuasion, I'm jamming good with Bed and Gearly.

26 July
The Skeletors dug us to their graves at The Purple Pit. Anorexic ambi-sexuals in white face, black tights, and ballet shoes found something they liked, and what they liked was The Blow Goes. Climbing on their seats, they gave us a standing ovation only muffled by their elegantly white-gloved hands. *Gone With The Show* moved a thousand streams in an hour, our new record.

27 July
Boyle said he'd lease us a shinky bullet-bus just like the Mantas', But it gets better; he's lined us up on a tour supporting Junki Pig. They're known for featuring up-and-comers who come up with something fresh, something like The Blow Goes *Meet Robo X*, a hypnotic spoken-word-with-bongos number Beddy and I are working on. Boyle said that, due to a last minute cancellation, they need a support band immediately.

"Welcome to the whirlwind," Boyle smiled as he handed us contracts.

"The Blow Goes will tour with Junki Pig at the request of the artists." read Boyle's press release. Nothing like starting at the top. Junki Pig's downloads nip at the Mantas' and they're second only to Death Row Jethro, whose popularity will no doubt fade, with him being dead and all. That lot's got nothing on us Blow Goes. Our steely determination will drive us onward, "To the toppermost of the poppermost," as Beddy puts it.

NME reviewed our live show at the Purple Pit, *Tsunamis of reverb echoed through a sonic hurricane that turned jades into fans by the first song's fade.*

Melody Maker tumbled for us too, *The Blow Goes' psychedelic soundscapes are spiked with surrealist lyrics expressing their unique brand of shoe gaze humour.* I was dead chuffed that they mentioned my lyrics so I showed it to Beddy. He scanned the page and scowled, "Toss this rubbish. We just have to mean it, man."

Major Boyle says he can free me from my halfway house obligation. As much as I'll miss wiping down miles of steel counters while cleaning fumes tickle my nose, it's time to move on.

30 July
Played our first show with Junki Pig. We Blow Goes went down a storm, eventually. Being second on the bill means the audience sat on their hands awaiting their beloved Junki Pig—at least until we got our groove on.

We commanded the stage.
We struck power chords.
We leaned into our mics.
We strained our neck muscles.
We sang for our supper.
We are The Blow Goes
And we mean it, man.

After bashing out *A Hole in The Planet,* we rocked *Wind Me Up.* Gearly shouted the coda while he segued a Mellotron string break into *Charing Cross Station*, a chug-a-lug surf-guitar trance he and Beddy wrote. "Don't leave gaps between songs," Beddy says. "Leave 'em breathless."

"Steady on lads." Beddy tempered our high after the show. He's well aware that swollen egos have wrecked many bands, but that can't happen with The Blow Goes—we've arrived pre-wrecked.

Last night, motoring along in our Bullet-Bus as the others played games or watched vids, I sat beside minder Bette wearing her busman's hat. She poured orange-spice tea from a thermos and we sang sea chanteys staring out at a spooky, moonlit motorway zooming by fast enough to blur.

I unrolled MemBrain and typed a reply to a journo who asked me to describe The Blow Goes' sound. *The Blow Goes blow hot and cold with a stripped-down, bi-polar sound mixing oboe d'amour, electric sitar, Theremin, Mellotron, and rain stick chorus arranged to evoke feelings of madness, love, and redemption with notes of wet corduroy and cardamom.* I wrote.

I read it to Bette and she laughed, "Why'd you give 'em a smart ass answer?"

"Don't like to explain my work. Does any artist? The part you can't describe is what makes it worthwhile. So why talk about it? Bedford dodges interviews entirely. He says, 'Music speaks for itself. Or it doesn't. And if it doesn't, it doesn't matter."

Miss Lilly's *Course in Confidence* advises me not to worry about nonessentials, not to indulge on stage nervousness, to stay cool and remember the audience wants to love you. Staying cool is easy when I glance over at Beddy pummeling his kit like the ghost of Keith Moon and we lock on rhythms good and tight.

It's a blast that all's going well with the band, but keeping the secret about mankind's origins feels like hiding an atom bomb in my pants. I could time a revelation to throw some heat on my book, but that might overshadow my subtle insights and wise sayings.

Food books sell. Perhaps I should write *A Bachelor's Guide to Cheese* and spill the beans about humanity's origins between praising the spidery veins in a tangy Gorgonzola and advice on eating rinds of Brie?

I watched a BBC doc about our melted poles and got inspired to pen a lyric I titled *Nanook, The Human Candle*.

A sickly glow lights his floe
It melts his house of ice
And blackens his carvings in bone
But Nanook's too clever to burn
Made himself a fireproof suit
Out of a white man's parachute

Later, lying in my bunk and nodding off, Jelly called, sounding grim. Fearing that she wanted to ask for something I didn't want to give, I cut it short, claiming an incoming call.

7 August

Major Boyle's promo is working. Our *Gone With The Show* Ep tracks massive streams, so he treated us to dinner with a champagne toast. Afterwards, buzzed on bubbly, we grabbed instruments and jammed a swamp thing. Gearly sung my *Nanook* lyrics as his Mellotron strings sawed away to a loop of arctic winds stabbing icicles in time with Bedford's march-time beat. We recorded a finished track in five hours flat. I felt happy as Larry, but still, a leaden weight sags the shoulders of this man who knows too much. It's an offbeat I can't beat off with an attitude of gratitude, an atomic bulge so fat and throbbing, I'm amazed no one's noticed. Would the pressure lessen if I just confided in a single person, "Oh, by the way, our entire world's just a reality show for a bunch of ancient aliens?" Who can you trust with a secret like that?

Living up to his motto: The slowest mule is closest to the whip; Boyle made some fast moves and booked us to headline Havana's Che Guevara Hall. No band's ever reached the Che so quickly. This alone qualifies him for rock'n roll sainthood in my book.

I read up on how Cuba's repressive communism eventually collapsed. Governmental broadband restrictions proved to be its death knell. They couldn't control the flow of information.

Cuba opened to free enterprise with a difference, strictly banning multi-national corporations. Only local businesses were allowed. It was called "Capitalism with a bearded face." Cubans' ferocious embrace of free enterprise astonished those unacquainted with the islanders' resourceful nature. Though allowing no global enterprises on their shores, Cubans exercised no restraint in exporting their own businesses. Rapido, a formerly government-run string of cafés, sold franchises worldwide. The popularity of their Cuban sandwiches led to Rapido becoming the world's largest fast food chain.

Today at lunch Beddy sighed, "There's something wrong with a world where people idolize nutters like us."

"I agree, but I'm grateful they do." I chimed in.

Lots of girls about on tour. Gearly likes to bang the gong all night long. Got my pick of the harem too, but groupies don't float my boat. Bedford seems a private man in search of something real to call his own.

11 August
BBC Holo-News floated by as I strolled the quay in Miami:

An elderly Brixton widow was found stuck to her kitchen floor by the heat. Her feet swelled up in government issued rubber soles that became stuck to the linoleum due to a chemical reaction brought on by record-breaking temperatures. Neighbors found her days later. Authorities were forced to bury her with the linoleum still attached.

No doubt she's gone to a better place—I just hope it's air-conditioned.

Two days later, London temps hovered around freezing.

14 August / Havana, Cuba
Beddy, Gearly, and I enjoyed our ninety-mile hover ride from Miami to Havana, sipping mojitos while munching bug snacks under clear blue sky.

We docked and walked the plank to solid ground that felt weird after the motion of the ocean. A restored 1950 Chevrolet convertible taxi pulled up and we rode through Havana with its top down, a perfect introduction to aged Spanish architecture and lofty palms swaying in time to live music playing everywhere. We passed a street lined with sultry beauties bent over car hoods, showing off rounded rumps while flashing flirty smiles.

We're bunking at the San Miguel, a small wedding cake of a hotel just off the harbor. High-ceilinged vanilla-coloured walls topped with white crown moldings and cool, terra cotta floors finish a perfect picture of tropical elegance. My terrace shows off gorgeous views of their quay, called the Malecon. A fresh breeze blows in off the Caribbean barely held back by towering seawall built against rising seas, but it's already obsolete—larger waves frequently splash over. Our oceans have gotten too big for their britches.

Sat on my terrace sipping Havana Club rum and coke, I'm a budding rock star in a great band with cool mates. Somebody pinch me.

Writing on the road is a bitch goddess that doesn't give it up to me, but Beddy prefers it. After shows, he retires to his room and slaves over demos with obsessive focus. Maybe he's out to prove something to his old mates in the Black Mantas.

He played us his latest demo during dinner. A brooding melody built to a soaring hypno-sprawl that quieted down to a peaceful easy feeling I wished could last forever, convincing me more than ever that we Blow Goes are poised on the edge of something great. "Keep up this quality of work and you'll pull the chords that open the drapes of heaven," Major Boyle pontificated at dinner. Beddy looked at him like he was daft, but I think he's right.

16 August

Major Boyle introduced us to seasoned Cuban players: Jose on Spanish guitar, conga drummer Federico, and Esmerelda, a sexy marimba master. Bedford wants to jam and see what's shaking. The two geezers are old enough to have lived through both the end of the Communist era and the transition to New Era, as it's called. Esmerelda is a former beauty pageant winner who's quite the stunner.

We jammed loose and cool with the Cubans in the hotel ballroom. Bedford Vann wrapped our melodies about their rhythms while Gearly sang my lyrics. They're a well-oiled machine that fit us seamlessly. Esmeralda's amazing marimba work adds a wild new twist to our sound. Our tunes sounded even better with a Cuban accent. Beddy said he wants to jam with them at our Che show.

18 August

People constantly want your attention on tour, making it tempting to "medicate" oneself just to keep up. Miss Lilly's *Course in Confidence* tells me to live up to my own expectations and say bollocks to the rest.

Wardrobe mistress Jane sidled upside me after dinner, "Dunno if you've noticed, but Cuban Mary's crushing on you." As if to say, "but you'd be a fool to go for her." I dared to wonder if Jane fancied me herself. Mary's our liaison with Che Guevara Hall, a smoky beauty with twinkly brown eyes and a Cuban butt.

"Most beautiful women in the world, the Cubans," Beddy said after he met her.

"Better get it, just in case it doesn't come around again," advised Gearly.

Bedford Vann played us some new demos during breakfast. Obvious fact: his muse has her tongue down his throat. If he continues to write at this level our album will be a brick house indeed.

My concept for the album is melodies ala Mellotron punctuated by bongo beats, sweetened with electric sitar, and layered with reverb spy guitar. Beatnik raps would follow square dance call-outs in the codas. Or something like that.

We are The Blow Goes
We bring love, redemption, and sound fiscal policy
We are space invaders
We are momma poppa agitators callin' for you
Climbing a mountain of rhythmic goo
We blow red hot and blue
To every Eskimo, Irishman, and Jew
We are The Blow Goes
Have a nice day

19 August

Falling in love with Cuba. Loads of Americans about that seem to agree. But the yanks have always had a thing for Cuba. You've got to love someone very much to not speak to them for sixty years, especially someone as beautiful as Cuba.

Recognizing a make or break moment when he sees one, Boyle has booked us a long stay for rehearsing. No one's complaining.

Took a taxi to suss Che Guevara Hall, the scene of our next triumph. A bigger-than-life statue of Che stands on a marble plinth gazing skyward with ocean light dappling his handsome features. I strolled around the plaza thinking on all that's gone down, then returned to the hotel ballroom where we rehearsed for hours. "No substitute for rehearsing," Beddy said, and he's right again.

Back at my room, I ordered a mojito and sipped it gazing at the deep blue sea glittering below in full moonlight. It'd take a sick bastard to break this spell.

20 August

We rehearsed with the Cubans again and caught a groove that could make an audience dance 'til they drop.

The Latin rhythms give our sound a swing, an organic, dance feel that we dig mightily. Bedford has been proven right again. We plan to do a few numbers with them at our Che gigs.

22 August

Sad to report that my worst fears have come true and the Blow Goes have copped a flat on the Boulevard of Broken Dreams.

Even in his darkest hours Bedford had always maintained a spark of hope. Being abandoned at the starting gate to choke on losers' dust while your band runs away to become superstars would blow any geezer's mind, but I thought the Blow Goes success had given him a firm grip on things. Impressed by his recovery, Gearly had taken to calling him The Amazing Vet. But Bedford's resilience failed him this morning.

After a coffee Cubana on the terrace I re-entered my suite to find a note under the door. *Must leave earth now*. it read in Beddy's distinctive hand, *Don't wish to leave a mess. You lot carry on.*

It struck me cold: Beddy's off his meds. I ran to his room, rang the bell, and banged on the door. Nothing. Banged again. Rang his phone, no answer. Ran down the hall to our tour medic's door.

"Beddy's gone off the rails, Ken. He's threatening suicide." I handed him the note.

"Legally, there's nothing I can do unless he exhibits dangerous behavior."

"He wrote a fuckin' suicide note!" I shouted, "That doesn't qualify as dangerous behavior?"

"I could write a script for some Calmz."

Ken was acting far too casual. Dipping into the Calmz himself?

Took the lift to the lobby and asked the desk clerk if he could open Beddy's room. They said they couldn't do that. I showed the clerk the note and he handed me the key. I raced to Beddy's room. He wasn't there. I asked around. No one had seen him.

I plopped in a lobby chair to try texting. Sometimes he'll answer a text when he won't pick up his phone. No luck. What to do? As I finished tapping out my fifth text, Beddy shuffled into the lobby looking the worse for wear.

"Found your note, Beddy. Off your meds, are you?"

"Meds made me brain mushy. Cut 'em loose to sharpen up. Moods have been swinging, but at least I'm open to inspiration. Sorry about the note. I was on my way to retrieve it."

"No worries. But it's no good dodging the meds if that loosens your hinges like this."

Beddy grunted noncommittally.

"Far along with that new song?" I tried a cold segue as Beddy seems at his best relating to work. I wanted to leave this drama behind as soon as possible.

"I'm stuck in the mud." He said softly.

"Fancy a jam?"

He nodded.

"Let's go." I felt relieved.

"Best listen to my new demo and cop a feel first. I'll email a file."

Back at my room, I opened MemBrain and sat on the terrace, looking out at the sea. Bedford's rising melody sailed across oceanic swells of Mellotron strings sounding like the ache of living. MemBrain image-synched with majestic canyons that led to limitless plains of golden wheat waving in a gentle wind. A tack piano and tambourine would make perfect accompaniment for lyrics about a broken man cocking an eye open to love. All it needs are lyrics, reverbed guitar and a solid bass line. Inspired, I drank a shot of

Havana Club, hit repeat and danced about the room, happy as a loon.

I pushed pause and popped open a minibar mojito. Cued another listen and fell back on the bed feeling spin-dizzy. The sexy abandon of Beddy's tune felt like a lost night that you only regret because you can't repeat it. It would make a perfect start for our concept album of nutters crawling back from the edge.

I called Beddy and told him I wanted to scratch up some lyrics rather than jam straight away. I grabbed MemBrain to capture lightning before it ethered off, but no muse visited. I started typing gibberish to unstop the flow, but no go.

Felt like taking a break so I visited the lobby bar and had a quick drink.

I took the lift to my room listening to the Swinging Sitars ooze an easy-listening version of Deathrow Jethro's *The Shadow of Your Pile*.

Back in my room and feeling inspired, I put on Beddy's masterpiece and jammed a lyric inspired by Gearly's nickname for him.

Watch him roll by on chrome
The Vet is smooth; he's amazing
His wounds are all up front, he never ran
Says, I'm fine. I'll always cope
But he's sailed past all hope
Steady on rolls The Amazing Vet
But he isn't past security yet
Fighting dark thoughts, past all hope
He says I'm fine; I've just enough rope

It might work with Beddy's brooding minor chords. Moody bits always seem easiest to write.

Feeling keen to stay in and write, I scratched out a lyric for *With a Little Yelp from My End*. It's a gas. "I've a hard time taking seriously anyone who isn't funny," Beddy said once and I agree.

The way things are going we'll have enough tunes for an album soon.

30 August
No excellent soul is exempt from a mixture of madness. ~ Aristotle

Woke up, got up, showered, and joined the boys for breakfast.

Beddy was his usual quiet self. I asked what's on. He said there was, "nothing to get hung about." He seemed unnaturally calm, even for him. Is that a side effect of the meds or a side effect of going off the meds?

"Scientists say the universe depends on our observation for its existence," I said, randomly.

"Do Earthquakes stop if they don't get our attention?" He said, then admitted, "I'm falling behind, Fumbo."

I changed subjects again, "Have you seen that girl Jane lately?" He had, "Saw her with a bloke at the pub."

"Who was he?"

"No idea. Seemed quite chummy."

Hearing this twisted my pretzel but good. Who's that geezer Jane was with?

Took the lift to the gym, hopped on a gen-bike and pumped for half an hour listening to Junki Pig's *Tears of a Clone*. Big beats and a sweaty workout pumped the blues out while I earned enough energy creds to power keytar wanking that I enjoyed deep into the evening.

3 September

Beddy's tale of that mystery bloke he saw with Jane has gotten up my spout. I got it bad and that ain't good. Anyone who had a heart would understand if they saw her making the scene in a cat suit coloured tangerine. But it's not just her looks. She's smart, has a great personality, and the work ethic of a demon on speed. Jane works so fast she's all but invisible 'til you look down during an inseam measurement and see those freakishly big eyes staring up at you. But I keep my cool. I shield my mood ring.

Back at the room, I switched on *Pops On Top* and watched Jellybean Syndicate bang out their smash, *John Barry Beat*.

A nonsense rhyme, stuck on repeat
Surfs an echoed John Barry beat
Sung from a doorway down the street
This boat is full. So sorry, Pete

Jellybean Syndicate seemed hyped in their interview, interrupting each other and laughing maniacally. They're understandably chuffed on all that's happened for them, but Gearly says they're pissing it away on a cesium bender. That won't happen with The Blow Goes, not after what we've been through. Besides, we're already loaded on pharms. Beddy's not the only band member on meds—I'm sorted myself. A computer monitoring my serotonin up-take rate delivers doses. It sees a sinking line and shoots a booster, a mandatory condition for my release.

5 September

"Everything exists in opposition," Jelly called to tell me the news this morning.

"Is your negativity reaching cosmic proportions?"

"How's that?"

"Never mind."

"On/off, ying/yang, nothing moves without its opposite. Mighty Handsome Johnny told me so. I know you won't believe me, but he's actually quite brilliant. Says every single thing in the world's made of itsy bits constantly whirling about so fast they give the appearance of solidity, but are, in fact, actually more space than solid. He explained this last night while cuffing me to the bedpost."

"Million-year old boulders aren't moving." I said, ignoring the cuff reference; Jelly likes to wind me up.

"That's inside out." She frowned.

"Losing me now, Jell."

"Johnny said things only appear solid. Everything is energy." Jelly smiled smugly at her fresh command of atomic theory.

"Are opposable thumb screws necessary to teach this lesson?" I crocodiled.

"You wanker!" Jelly laughed. "I'm off. Ciao."

I put on *Listen to the Swarm*, kicked back on couchette and inhaled a needle-thin spliff a fan had slipped me. That proved a mistake when I saw a wall bulging outwards—at least I think it did.

"Raw meat," I shouted at the wall, now looking well behaved as all good plaster should be, "I will eat you with a fork and spoon should you so much as bulge a single bulge. You have been warned." Am I flipping out or just high? I will not go quietly into madness, not while on the cusp of rock stardom. It's a delicate balance having two nutters in a group—we're constantly on the edge of a creative breakthrough while flirting with commitment to a padded room playing twelve-hour games of *Stare Straight Ahead* with the ghost of Syd Barret.

Too knackered to undress, I flopped on the bed and conked out.

6 September
I like dreams of the future better than the history of the past. ~ Thomas Jefferson.

Agreed, Thomas.

At the end of his life, the pessimist might be proven right but the optimist will have enjoyed a better life. I like that one, too. Who said it?

I should contact Ms. Caruthers about re-starting that *Laffs for the Loo* book. A possible back cover blurb:

From the Queen Mum to Piccadilly clowns, everyone enjoys a good laugh in the loo and Fumbo's observations are guaranteed to tickle your funny bone when you need it most.

7 September
There's a tide in the affairs of men
That, if taken at the flood
Leads to fortune

Afternoon rehearsal went well enough. Bedford Vann hit a ride cymbal, Gearly twanged a spy guitar, I pounded my bass, and together we dug a mighty groove.

I scratched up some random lyrics. Gearly sang lead, laid on Theremin, added Mellotron horns and mixed it. In five hours we had a song so sweet that birds stopped singing to listen. That's what it's like when we're in the pocket. And getting in the pocket gets easier every time we play.

As for being a rock star, I can do this. All I need is to paddle my canoe through a wall of voodoo, clamber ashore, and hack a shining path through this darkened jungle 'til I stand on stage, rocking hard with my mates, The Blow Goes.

8 September

Woke up happy as Larry, strolled to an outdoor café and got sorted with a Cuban breakfast.

NME headline blared from a café tabletop: COMATEENS DIG THE BLOW GOES SOUND. Good on us— that lot's the point of the spear. But a sidebar brought things down, INFINITEENS CLAIM TOTAL INDIFFERENCE. Who cares about tossers who claim indifference to everything?

Alone in my room, I drank a double shot of Havana Club rum with soda and lemon, turned on keytar and jammed lyrics to a blue-beat track by Beddy.

I saw her in a video
Chased by a squidy-o
Called her Dirty Pretty-o
She looked so pretty
It made me feel dirty

10 September

Tonight proved to be our night of nights, our show of shows. As online headlines screamed, *The Blow Goes Play The Che*, play we did, and very well indeed.

We were all nerves backstage waiting for our Cuban amigos to finish their set. Gearly did an impromptu round of corny jokes that forced a few weak laughs, but didn't help much.

On stage at last, we were so hyped we flew through our opening number *Cluster Pain* too fast. But a warm wave of love washing over us soon relieved our tension. The rest of the show rolled by like a dream as I locked bass lines with Beddy's machine gun rhythms and we flew through space and time together.

Mid-show, we brought our Cuban friends on to play songs we'd rehearsed. The audience went mad.

After the Cubans left the stage to a standing ovation, we rocked on like a hurricane. We'd become a band at last, a great band at that. The audience agreed, applauding wildly throughout our set, honored us with a standing ovation at the end and demanding an encore.

We gave them *Something in The Air*, an ancient hit that Beddy likes, originally by Thunderclap Newman.

11 September
After all the work preparing for our first big show, we decided to stay on in Cuba for a few days relaxation.

12 September
Bed looked shaky over breakfast when he said, "I need a break." When I asked him what that meant in terms of the band, he just grunted and waved me off.

I taxied to the beach, sat on a bench and stared at the sea, thinking about what's going on. Are we Blow Goes fishermen hauling in a prize catch or sucker fish nibbling at a barbed hook?

Jelly texted to say, *Laying here starkers, thinking on you, Mr. F.* Am animated emoji proved her claim true. She got me going, but why?

Sure you didn't hit the wrong number?

This is rock star Ignatius Fumbo, isn't it?

Peek behind her curtain, you'll find another curtain.

Have to admit you take a pretty picture, Jell, what's on?

Are illegals screwing with her mind? I had no time to figure. Major Boyle rang through requesting an emergency meeting.

"I don't need to tell you what's on with the band, Fumbo." he said, "You boys have proven you have the stuff to spin big wheels. If there was any doubt, your show at the Che proved it. And now the world knows. Major buzz is building, but Bedford's uncertainty threatens to stop things cold. A whole album of quality tracks like those you've done is what the world needs now. You lot will make history if you can stay focused. I love the man like a brother and I know you do, too. Crazy to bust up the band when you've got momentum like this."

"It would be barmy to blow this opportunity." Boyle repeated. He knows his business; he got no argument from me.

"First think has to be on Beddy's health." I said, having no clue where Boyle was taking things.

"Let's give him a few days and see how it goes," he said. "We've little choice. Blow Goes have got a buzz other bands would kill for and you haven't even released an album yet."

Feeling anxious, I took my ukulele to the pool, sat in a chaise, and ordered a mojito. After a few sips, Jane pulled up in a black bikini and flip-flops with a gossamer scarf tied about her waist as skirt.

She stopped to listen, so I improvised a lyric.

Do-re-mi dinero,
Mama you bonafide-o
Call me a fool
Sitting here by the pool
But I love me a doe-eyed doe
Re-mi dinero

I finished with a flamenco flourish and slapped that uke on its ass. She laughed. She clapped. She smiled.

"Sorry, no encores."

"None requested, sir."

Her cheeks flushed. My lip sweated.

We'd had a moment at last. She looked startled, gave me a peck and turned to walk inside, "Sketches due in the morning," she explained, "Thanks for the concert."

Feeling stirred up with nowhere to go, I took the lift upstairs and showered. An ad projected in the shower stall sounded good, so I auto-taxied to FreeBubble, said to be built for Cuba's downtrodden masses as the island's economy struggled with the transition from communism to capitalism. Of course, as a budding rock star I can afford the very best of bubbles, but FreeBubble claims to have its own funky charms. Sadly, they were lost on me. It was novel, but a hovel and the smell of poverty brought me down fast. Fellow attendees were a desultory lot of native Cubans and a few sucker tourists like me who respond to ads in our showers until we tire of touring rusty Russian submarines and smelly bubbles. I booted the antidote and left early.

Sitting on the terrace, watching a red ball sun tint the fat bottoms of low-hanging clouds cherub pink over azure Caribbean waters, I thought about what a lucky git I am, and how well the band's jelling now that I'm on bass. I'm still stumped on how to move forward without Beddy. How do you help a man who trips and falls on the stairway to heaven? Everything's going great for us, but it's lost on him. When I asked how he felt at lunch, he was typically elliptical, "I'm happy about the band and all, but nothing else makes sense."

For supper, I ordered room service pizza with basil, goat cheese and mushrooms and sat on the terrace to enjoy the sunset, immediately spotting Jane walking the quay with some bloke. Pretending not to notice, I distracted myself studying random select options on MemBrain.

I didn't like seeing Jane with that geezer, not one bit. Is he the same bloke Beddy saw her with?

15 September

Major Boyle called a lunch meeting.

"Albert Hall, gentlemen, is booked. Don't have to tell you what this means."

Gearly looked dumbstruck. Bedford stared at his plate, but thought I saw him crack a smile.

"A spot opened up when Dark Matter was forced to cancel due to their bassist croaking on a vomit comet. The press from your Che gig is proving quite powerful."

It's all very exciting, but an unspoken question hung heavy in the jubilant air: What if Beddy drops out?

Needing distraction, I caught The Rude Lovers at Bulb Edison. Lead singer Tracey Deluxe belted songs with a raspy conviction that made me a believer.

I made a play for popular appeal
Just to feel how that feels
It feels like napalm
It feels like an A-Bomb
Knowing what we were in for
We laughed and laughed some more
Angels like you, all legs and wings
Don't know the trouble you bring

Back at the flop, I clicked an E-Card from Jelly, *Missing you much, Fumbsy. Broke off with boyo for GOOD this time*. She attached a riff that twanged my MemBrain's speakers with lonesome motorway guitar.

It felt funny, how little I cared. But seeing Jane with that geezer itches my wig. What's their deal?

22 September / Miami, Florida

Major Boyle booked us flops at the New Delano Hotel at South Beach, Miami, Southern States of America. The joint's as swanky as King Tut's hut with a breezy lobby lined with gossamer, two-story tall curtains billowing in soft tropic breezes. The lobby stretches straight through from front door to beach sand. It's a shame about the advancing sea forcing their move inland. Must have put a damper on things when the South seceded as "The world's newest nation!" and immediately suffered through a non-stop series of climate disasters.

We're here to shoot a vid and an advert. Major Boyle calls it a working holiday, but I fail to see the holiday aspect, unless being surrounded by sunburnt tourists while we sweat our arses off running around in soggy beach sand qualifies.

A bouquet of exotic flowers were waiting in my room with this note:

Welcome to Miami, Mr. Fumbo.
Thought you might like some colour in your tent.

Jane's bouquet sent out an aroma of undefined love. I flopped on the bed and lie there smiling at the ceiling.

Gearly huddled over his MemBrain during the flight over, mixing tracks like a madman across the water. He's laid down a tough wall-of-sound sounding like Bowie's *Diamond Dogs*. The bones of an album are poking through, but nobody's said the "a" word yet.

I sat on the terrace to email thanks to Jane and my muse breathed heavily, inspiring this tribute to Death Row Jethro, reflecting his love of 1970s Americana.

White Trash And I'm Proud
(Anthem for a doublewide life)
Johnny borrowed Candy's last dinero
Counted it out on the hood of her Camaro
Shot her lunch with a bow and arrow
Johnny's house might be narrow
And made of tin, but it's mobile
Johnny's poor, but proud and noble

He sings it loud
I'm white trash
And I'm proud
Johnny's got a long-range plan
Gonna take some money from the man
He'll pay Candy back and move in with them
Candy and the kids will hear him when
Johnny sings it loud
I'm white trash
And I'm proud
He sings it's allowed
To be white trash
And proud
Johnny went to see the gypsy
She gave him a green light
But the man guarded his money
Guarded it tight
Guarded it from a guy named Johnny
Johnny sings it loud
I'm white trash
And I'm proud
He sings it's allowed
To be white trash
And proud
(Repeat chorus as fade)

A tribute to the newest star in hillbilly heaven I recorded over a simple keytar bass line and a drum loop from Bedford Vann.

The "A" word has officially broken cover. Major Boyle called us to an evening meeting to discuss the album. There's no turning back from history now. We batted thematic ideas around. Beddy suggested a rock opera of crack-up and redemption he calls *Lord of the Strings*. Gearly wants to layer Mellotron strings atop a wall of guitar reverb to score a tribute to genetic research titled *Send In The Clones*. I mentioned my idea of combining wah-wah keytar and gospel choruses with electric sitar, but didn't have a theme in mind. I favor Beddy's concept, but not his title.

The meeting went well. Nobody's self-importance got in the way. We've all been through too much for that.

Songs under consideration for the album:
1. *We are The Blow Goes* (abstract vocal harmonies with mysterioso Mellotron strings)
2. *With a Little Yelp From My End*
3. *A Hole in The Planet* (theme for Deathrow Jethro)
4. *Nanook* (with arctic wind effect)
5. *The Amazing Vet*
6. *Dirty Pretty*
7. *Pretty Dirty*
8. *White Trash And I'm Proud* (Anthem for a double-wide life)
9. *Dust to Dust in an Afternoon* (a pocket symphony exploring life's fleeting nature)

This album should ring some fucking bells or my name's not Ignatius Quintan Fumbo III. Still, there's massive work to do if we're going to haul this monster to the zoo.

Walking on water wasn't built in a day.
~ Jack Kerouac

That's an undeniable fact, Jack. I slammed four shots of reposada tequila with water chaser and drunk-dialed Jane.

"I was just nodding off," she yawned.

"We'll talk later, then."

"No worries, just off the phone with my brother."

"Oh yeah? Where's he?"

"New York. He's a journo covering a squatters' riot in the simulated meat packing district. Didn't I introduce you when he visited me in Cuba?"

Her brother must be the bloke Beddy and I spotted her with in Havana. Her brother! I fell asleep smiling.

29 September
Woke up to an email shouting in blood red Gothic: *Don't get me wrong. I'm your biggest fan. But you lot need to get off yer arses and release some content.*

Agreed. I wrote back. *Just hang on. Big things come to those who wait.*

He answered instantly, *Look into the eyes of your audience and you'll see forest wolves changing our minds ten times per second. Think we'll wait for the likes of you?*

Sounds like a tosser, but he's got a point. The Blow Goes must activate or stall out. We've got a solid start. Demos? Finished. Lyrics? Ready. Just need final recordings and overdubs, polishing, mixing, sequencing, and artwork, a general pulling together that takes time. Pushing our madness and redemption theme, Major Boyle's done well with promotion and media buzzes with anticipation.

Even Tricky Dick's going down a storm. He's proven to be a great hook for media coverage. Major Boyle's going to put a *Tricky Dick Approved* seal on our merch. Sent out a press release saying we're making a donation to The Monkey Mansion with each piece of merch sold, dedicated to establishing a proper habitat for Dick's furry cousins.

We shot a vid for *Dirty Pretty* on the beach at golden hour. Between takes, I watched Jane do her grueling job as wardrobe mistress with multiple costume changes, plodding through sand to attend details, with the hurry-up-and-wait of a shoot. She rocked it with blushing cheeks and a smile. After we wrapped, I watched her ankle off the set. She caught me staring, but I failed to cop.

After a dinner with the crew, I conked out listening to Bitmap Bossa Nova's *Stranger That's a Bore*.

30 September
Couldn't believe my eyes when Bedford's press release popped up on MemBrain this morning:

Happy to see The Blow Goes blowing up big, but need some personal time to sort things out. Hope the boys will carry on and have every faith they will. Don't wish to hold them back as they deserve every success that's bound to come their way.

Considering our strong start, it's amazing how quickly things turned pear-shaped in tropical heat. Boyle will have to cancel our Albert Hall gig. And suddenly our album is a dead fish drying on a beach with gulls picking flesh off its ribcage.

Gearly and I talked over tea. He's equally clueless about how to help Bedford, especially frustrating when the tracks we've got are a creamy blend of rock steady beats, good intentions, and wafts of patchouli in a psychodrama of crack-up and redemption as Beddy suggested. Mixed with Beddy's rock-steady beats, Gearly's mixing magic, and my beatnik lyrics, it's sure to melt minds. But what's left for us without Bedford Vann, music to pound coffin nails by?

1 October
Wearing red silk pyjamas, Jane brushed by me in the hall last night. She gets me going every time. Back in my room, I raised a glass of absinthe to a most mysterious miss. If I were her, I'd kiss me.

Gearly and I discussed things over breakfast and decided that all we can do is let Beddy rest and hope for the best.

2 October
A cashmere pendulum swings down the darkened canyons of my mind.

With Bedford missing in action, I've become the band's default authority. Used to laugh at spoiled rock stars' gripes, but not now with a band member missing in action, a stillborn album hanging around our necks, and gigs scheduled with no clue how to fulfill them.

Major Boyle had us all fully scanned in case something like this came up. Beddy's cool with us doing what we have to, even if that means finishing the tour with a replibot of him. Boyle said he's having one programmed now. It'll play samples of Beddy's actual beats, but will no doubt, prove a poor substitute; drum machines have no soul.

Does Bedford Vann Fear Success? A NME headline screamed our troubles, but the buzz keeps building, regardless. Beddy wants us to press on and grab our tide at the flood. We've decided to keep his problems secret 'til we see how things go.

Knackered by stress, I fell asleep instead of going out.

3 October
Giving someone advice is like trying to steer a car with your voice.

Writing this high above the Atlantic on our return to London. Bedford elected to stay behind in Miami for some R&R. We all hope that marinating in tropic air will do him some good.

Vid-phoning Jelly from the plane, I could almost smell the stale piss and greasy chips in the dingy Soho pub where she answered. A nasty-looking geezer in neoprene vest, welder's goggles, and porkpie hat with a bullet-band sat beside her with his arm clamped tightly about Jelly's bony shoulder. Would she be with him if he didn't offer illegals?

Vibrating with chemical energy, Jelly rapped in strung-out staccato,

"HelloFumbothishere'sStanley.DidyouknowthatNazisinventedUFOsFumboIknowyoudon'tbelievemebutit'strueandtheyflythemfromdeepinsidetheEarthatthenorthpoleandStanleysayswecangothereandlookfortheirholeintheiceso we'regoingreckonyouwannacome, too?"

I couldn't handle seeing her so pranged out, "Just checking in, Jell. Bad reception. I'll ring you later."

What can you say to help someone who's deranged?

4 October / London, England
Major Boyle booked us rooms at the Savoy, quite posh digs for a geezer outta H-Block Subsidized. But with my mood ring spinning midnight blue, shinky digs mean very little.

He brought our new Bullet-Bus by for inspection. It was nicely kitted with kitchen, mini-theater and exercise gear, but I couldn't get excited without Beddy around to share it.

Wondering how he might be getting on, I opened my email to find an answer:

Hello Fumbo,

Life's a breeze here by the sea. Amazing how quickly I've mastered the art of beachcombing. Latest finds include a sand-frosted glass bottle with Chinese markings, two perfect conk shells I'm playing tunes on, a scorched fishing float hinting of tragedy at sea, and a

*styro chest bearing a soggy surprise. So you see, I've
been keeping busy. How're things on your end?*
Always your drummer,
Bedford

Beddy seems satisfied with life as a stranger on the
shore. I just hope it's a temporary thing.

Spent the day trying to conjure up lyrics, but felt
edgy and unable to concentrate. Frustrated, I wanted to
spin my mind off, so I taxied to Amperage Nocturne, a
daft disco, but it's a scene. Built as a sphere on stilts
with a ramp spiraling to a top deck, its holos of planets
and stars spin as a backdrop for beautiful people to
dance and flirt.

A stately African doorman with scarified face and
mirrored chrome derby nodded recognition as he
motioned me inside without charge. "Always welcome,
Mr. Blow Goes," he replied. Geezers recognized me
straightaway, backslapping me on The Blow Goes'
success. A gangly bloke wearing a stovepipe hat
expressed sympathy about our well-publicized dilemma
with Bedford. Meant well, but reminded me of
something I was there to forget. I chatted with fans,
signed a few girls' body parts and drank one too many
Death in The Afternoons.

I thought a stroll back to the hotel might sober me
up. It didn't. I'm lying on a spinning bed, with a queasy
stomach and thinking about picking up my keytar, but
that seems like far too much effort.

5 October

Had breakfast by a window at the hotel café, hoping
that might ease my hangover. I gazed out of a rain-
spotted window at soggy London while sipping a double
cappuccino and thought up a shinky new title for my
book of wisdoms: "What's The Worry Up in Here?" A
swinging combination of affirmations, bittersweet
wisdoms, and easy recipes for singles-on-the-go written
in Benzedrine Kerouac style couldn't miss. It might
include Blow Goes tunes, comic asides, self-help
cartoons, and easy-to-make recipes.

I've been missing Sparky Fuego's crooked smile and
irresistible laugh. Having lived his own dumbstruck

days, he might have an idea on how to pull Beddy out of his tailspin. It's way past time we visited, in any case.

I didn't want to pull up all posh, so I took the tube to Sparky's squat in Hunger City, an upper class bastion destroyed in a food riot. It's been repurposed as a maze of cobbled-together squatters' shacks with ribbed metal walls, do-it-yourself solar cells, and smelly porta-potties. Who would have thought such a posh neighborhood could become a nightmare carnival of oxidized lorries, busted-up shipping containers, and wheel-less buses right in the midst of London?

Dotted with smoldering fires smelling of burnt rubber and desperation, Hunger City more than lived up to its rep. I dodged rusting auto parts half-buried in mud amid puddles of glowing, florescent chemicals giving off fumes that stung my beak. Off in the distance, a solo clarinet bleated *Rhapsody in Blue*.

Sparky told me to look for a billboard wrap showing Mystery Girl draped over the bonnet of a Nissan Cilantro. Didn't spot it right off, but I did see one that for an insurance company that asked, *What's most important to you?* Someone had spray-painted *FOOD!* as an answer.

I passed a yurt with a homemade banner advertising *A Fortune Teller When You Need One*. A gypsy woman sat out front on a campstool, waving hello. Wavy hair and waxy red lips dominated her weathered face. I waved back and kept moving.

After trudging aimlessly through a muddy maze for half an hour, I spied a billboard vinyl showing Mystery Girl's come-hither pose enhanced with marker-pen mustache and monocle. A cracker box palace of packing crates was ram-shackled about a crumbling red brick chimney with the vinyl serving as a roof. A hand-lettered sign told me I'd found him.

SPARKY FUEGO HERE
Opinions Given - Lowest Rates

I knocked on a rusty, bullet-holed car door. Its spidery-cracked window jerked down with a dry, scraping sound and Sparky poked his bushy ginger noggin out to stare straight through me for an ice-cold second. When he recognized me and broke out that irresistible toothy grin, the world turned right again.

"Well, if it isn't Ignatius Fumbo! I do declare. Welcome to Fuego Manor House. Come in. Come in, friend. No charge for you."

"You're a sight for sore eyes, Sparky." I stepped into a small room with rusted metal walls smelling of boiled cabbage and loneliness. Sparky's pale blue eyes twinkled in flickering light from a small trash fire smoldering in a massive brick fireplace.

"You're looking good. How's Bedford?" Sparky cut straight to the point.

"Not so good, Sparky. He's come unhinged lately, perhaps due to our workload. We've got a major buzz going and that's brought pressure. Anyway, whatever the cause, he's quit the band."

"Bedford's a tough nut to crack. Never knew a geezer with a harder shell wrapped around a softer yolk."

Sparky invited me to take a seat on an upturned metal bucket beside a car bonnet lid serving as coffee table. He left for a moment and returned with steaming cups of tea.

"Hard to believe that he's folding up when things have been going so well for you lot."

"Ideas, Sparky? Something that might help him?"

"Too bad he can't just stand back, get some perspective and refuse to take it so seriously. Music's supposed to be fun—and this is the chance of a lifetime. Sorry if I spout a bundle of cliché's. Just wish I had a clue about how to help." Sparky turned wistful. "I'll think on this."

"No worries. It's just good to see you, mate. We might have an opening for a roadie if you're interested. We're obligated to do a tour with or without Bedford."

"I'd be happy to help, most happy indeed."

Reminiscing about Haversham's, Sparky and I fell about laughing like I hadn't done since leaving the Farm. While he fetched another pot of tea, I slipped a hundred pound cred code into a Rover hubcap serving as ashtray on the mantle.

I didn't like leaving Sparky behind in that smelly pit, not one bit. Staring at my glum pan reflected in a tube car window, I decided to find him a spot on our crew. He'll be good for morale.

Stopped at Red Lion pub where I got pissed on lager 'n limes while listening to jukebox sounds of Death Row Jethro, George Huffman, Simpletones, Rude Lovers, Spoiler, T-Rex, Amphetamine Gazelle, Dylan Dray, and Joe Meek classics. My hostile vibe kept any fans away.

I staggered back to the Savoy and flopped, pissed as hell. I don't recall ordering the spinning bed upgrade, but there it was and I couldn't figure how to turn it off. Putting my leg on the floor to stop it only made things worse.

6 October

Woke up. Got outta bed. Felt the bone inside my head, a hangover courtesy of yesterday's shanties. It's the sugar that does you in. Room service cappuccino and chocolate croissant brightened things.

I sat on the terrace, switched on my Theremin and got hung up in a loop that reminded me of when all this used to be fun. I loaded it onto MemBrain, layered Gearly Mellotron strings onto a Bedford bongo loop, added French horns and a plucked harp pizzicato. Voila, an instrumental was born. Its minor key reflects my mood, but gave it a romantic title: *Sunset on Mars*.

Our minder Mal called to say *Cluster Pain has* hit number one. That called for a drink.

"Dead chuffed, Mal. Have you told Beddy?"

"He's dead chuffed, too."

"How's he been?"

"Seems happy enough since he got back on the meds. Still showing little interest in music, though."

Is the medicated Buddha Bedford his true self or is the true Bedford the mood swing king, morose and suicidal, then flying high the next day? Should I be happy he's calm or worried he's a zombie? Colour me confused. In any case, our album will curdle up and die if he can't help us finish it.

Writing a book might prove a good distraction at a time like this, but what kind of book? If it's sales you want most, write a cookbook. But I can't boil an egg, so that's out. Science fiction might work, or I could combine the two and write a cookbook of dishes suitable for an alien invasion.

A science fiction cookbook would be a perfect hybrid revealing the secret of mankind's origins. Coming on as fantasy, it would pivot to unmask its factual basis in the midst of a blancmange recipe.

Meanwhile, Blow Goes' wheels sink deeper into quicksand each day. A tough go, but our only alternative is surrender. Gearly and I must finish the album, with or without our favorite drummer.

9 October / A forward slash

Sat across the crew table from Jane at breakfast, "Got a comp ticket for Bubble People tonight."

"Good on ya." She smiled. I couldn't tell if she was being sweet or snide.

"Got an extra, too." I was hoping she'd bite.

"Yes," she said, cracking a smile with her sexy, toothy mouth, "I'd love to go."

Happiness.

Bussed to Pinewood Studios to shoot endorsements for daft Mega products: PockeTan and RotoRoma. We Blow Goes are instant whores: just add money.

I returned to the hotel, showered, and met Jane in the lobby: a perfect girl in a dress cut just low enough to present porcelain white breasts rising like suns above a fitted, scarlet red cocktail dress, flats, and glowing antenna headband pulsing with harmonious waves of warmth and empathy.

We taxied to the Palladium where Bubble People planned a release party for their new album, *Surfactant Slump*. It doesn't seem up to the level of *Pandemonium Panorama*, but might need to listen more. Patented four-part harmonies swung sweet as angels. Players stood on different levels of a scaffold fronted with light bars changing colours in time with the beats.

We taxied back to the hotel. "Sorry to run, but I've sketches to finish," Jane sighed as goodbye. It's always about the sketches. I left her at the hotel entrance and walked on down the street.

An ad for Blunder Bubble floated by: Roll up that MemBrain and party hearty at Blunder Bubble, a topsy-turvy world where everything's a mistake. High on stimis from the Bubble People show, I wanted a laugh and thought I'd give it a go.

Headlines floated above as I walked.

SPACE JUNK SINKS BOAT
MISSING TOT FOUND INSIDE PUMPKIN:
SURVIVED ON SEEDS, PULP

Blunder Bubble claimed to be a real laffro dazzler, but the funny rolled off without a trace. Nice thing about having a fat load of creds, I can ditch a bum bubble any time without worry.

I walked across the street to Beauty Bubble, but it let me down, too. I wasn't in the mood for a candyfloss world of lemonade lakes and treacle trees. Overdosed on glucose, I split in ten. On the way out, I saw an ad for Irony Bubble and popped in for a laugh, but it wasn't the kind of irony I was expecting. Instead, it was a dark world of massive, rusty golem clanking with menace. Steely jaws slammed shut to industrial Goth pounding heavily from overhead gargoyle speakers. I split in five. Got enough rusty darkness clanking inside already, thanks.

Returning to the hotel, I greeted Tricky Dick, fetched him some water and food, and switched on telly to watch a critic slag off a new surreality show from The Southern States of America, *Call Me Adam Ape*. I thought Dick might enjoy it, so I turned the TV 'round so he could watch from his bed in the corner.

What kind of world are we living in when our most popular entertainment is watching a monkey assume the monarchy of The Southern States of America? I mean, a bleeding hairy ape set loose to run what was once (part of) the world's most powerful nation? America's southern states might be bankrupt, but must they embrace their failure so feverishly? Adam Ape sweated, pounded the table, and raged purple. Tricky Dick loved it, especially when they showed a clip of the presidential monkey trashing the Oval Office. This sent Tricky Dick

166

into a fit. He ran around like a nut and threw my collectable Stu Bilat tea mug to the floor, shattering it beyond repair.

I cleaned it up as I watched.

How quickly things crumbled for the most successful, powerful nation in history. Sadly, it's a pattern as old as pride.

Pay-per-view cablecasts are a dodgy solution to the S. S. A.'s insolvency. Planting stink bombs during sessions of congress and broadcasting the fun live was fine, but crowning a chimp as king? I don't like the way that rolls out.

The phone rang, "Mr. Fumbo?"

"Here."

"David Slant."

"Okay?"

"I'm a producer with iTV. I hope you've a minute to talk. There's something I have to discuss with you."

"And that is . . ."

"I understand you found a hold-all at the Teletemple cafeteria some months back . . ."

"Not saying yes or no."

"Well, frankly, we bear responsibility for that. It was a plant for our programme, *Lost and Floundering*. Have you seen our show, Mr. Fumbo?"

"Not on my schedule."

"We leave provocative things about for people to find, then record their reactions. It's great fun. But it doesn't always work, as in your case with the secret of mankind's origins and all. We've been tracking you for months, waiting for you to do something funny. Frankly, with the single exception of your crab-like run to the loo when you found the hold-all, you've been a bit of a disappointment."

"Sorry, mate. Don't know what your game is, but this one's real. I had to crack Teleternity codes in order to read it."

"*Lost and Floundering* is a production of the Teleternity Network. We knew you had a security rating and you'd be able to crack your way in. Those codes were changed instantly after you gained access. It was all a set-up."

"Really? The whole thing's a joke?"
"Terribly sorry if we've upset you."
"Oh, that's quite alright. It's a relief, actually."
"A relief" is putting it mildly. I was ecstatic.

11 October

Now that I'm no longer shouldering the burden of
revealing mankind's origins, I'll go back to plan A and
write "Up in Here You'll Find Wisdom's Glittering
Treasure" as a self-help book based on ancient wisdoms.
Old quotes might seem musty, but they've lasted
because they contain eternal power.

Insomnia's a common curse, perhaps if I design the
book to inspire nods, it might sell even better? "Mama
Said Knock You Out, So Get Up in Here And Nod Off"
could bind soporific homilies in a softly padded cover
serving as a handy pillow. I can see the ad copy now:
*Desperately seeking a kip? This book will change the
way you sleep, one page at a time.*

Staring out at clear blue sky with symphonic musical
accompaniment by Listen to The Swarm, I texted Jane,
*Come over now and I'll let you watch a Death Row
Jethro vid*, an obvious joke as birds universally hate the
bluster king.

I rang Bedford, "How're you feeling?"
"On and off. You?"
"Lots to do with the Royal Albert gig back on." I
wanted to draw him out about the band, but he didn't
take the bait. I pressed, "Feel like working on the
album?"
"Silence is golden," said the Bed.
"What's that? I couldn't hear you." I replied. He
knew I'd heard and raised a laugh that rattled my china,
a good way to end the call.

I thought on Jelly and how far she's fallen, but I'd
rather think on Jane slinking upside me with her soft
round parts pushing silk about, tilting up for a kiss with
her phaser set to stun. Might have been a psychic
transmission as she rang up just then in answer to my
invitation, "Vids sound good."

I hung up and played The Bod Squad's *God Save
The Spleen* as a tidying up soundtrack. As I was

finishing there was a knock on the door. I opened it on Jane sublimely decked in a sparkly cat suit topped with a ladybug red white polka-dot peplum jacket and silver go-go boots. Dark brown, bone-straight hair set off her doll-like face and ruby red lips. With a platinum-tipped fringe framing her giant eyes, she looked like the world's cutest anime' heroine come to life.

I wolf whistled.

"Something I just whipped up. Look alright?"

I looked her up and down while crooning Barry White syle, "Uh, huh, yeah baby." She laughed and my mood ring lit up like the sun.

We got through half a Death Row Jethro vid before starting to make out. I switched off the screen and clicked on Groupo Pluto's *Moon Moods to Make You Misty* as we laid on the bed French-kissing and groping for zippers.

We stopped briefly to clink glasses in a toast to everything and nothing, then sipped champagne listening to slinky beats. Our kisses turned wanton and I pushed her back on the couch. She giggled and fought back with surprising strength. I let her wrestle out from under me, then pinned her down caveman-style as we copped a major laughing fit.

I slipped a mitt down Jane's knickers. She slid my trousers off and freed my steely pole from the land o' cotton. I stood, gathered her in my arms and carried her to the bed, a caveman on a mission. We made love and floated back to earth.

I said I was thirsty. She said, "Me too," and fetched a glass of water.

We listened to Oboes of Delhi featuring the wah-wah sitars of Fada Raj as we spooned to sleep. Sunlight beaming in woke us early. I accidentally rang room service when I tried to push the button to shut the shade. We were starved so we ordered breakfast.

Hearing a knock from room service. Jane pulled on my pajama top. We sat in bed and gorged on bug crumpets, tea, and jam then jumped on each other for another sweaty go.

Jane rose to leave, "My, my, Mr. Fumbo, Room 202 certainly does have its charms. I must drop by more often."

As soon as she left, I grabbed MemBrain and pecked out a lyric 'til the blower interrupted.

"Hello. Is this Fumbo Ignatius?"

"Yes, and this is?"

"Bram Van De Camp of Big S Little S Media here. Your interview in OK GO! Inspired us to think your story might pile up quite well as an e-book. Would you like to talk with us about that?"

"Possibly."

"We'd like to frame it as an autobiography."

"I keep a diary."

"Mind allowing us a peek?"

12 October

"It's My Party And It's A Freak-Out", would make a provocative title for an autobiography of good times and bad with no holds barred, including my doomed romance with Jelly, daft Haversham's days, and stymied musical ambition.

Autobiographies only work if you cop to the truth. Who wouldn't enjoy reading about a mental case on the dole that becomes a world-class rock star and falls in love with the world's most mysterious woman? Proposed jacket blurb: *An unbelievable, but true tale of a mental case who becomes a rock and roll hero. Thrill to his journey from locked-down nutter to world-class star.*

It would help if we finished the album so I could cross promote it with my book. But when will our album be finished? The trouble with bands is a built-in dependence on others when others are undependable. Solo acts like Johnny Zhivago have it made. Maybe that's the way to go?

Jelly texted, confessing her increased consumption of illegals. *The trouble started when I finally hooked up with Mighty Handsome Johnny. No excuses. Knew what I was getting into.* I called her, but she didn't pick up.

I decided to stay in.

Took the elevator to the lobby where I ran into Jane's assistant Samantha who asked if I wanted to have a cuppa. Sitting in the wood paneled hotel café, she copped to my scene with Jane. "She doesn't open up to people easily, but she's really keen on you, I've never seen her like this." As I listened, a text came through from Beddy:

In town, rested, and ready to rock.
Always your drummer,
Bedford

This is turning out quite a lucky day indeed. I left Samantha to meet him at his room.

"Feeling strong now, Fumbo."

"Best news ever. Feel up to making some noise?" I thought that playing might keep Beddy on track.

"Let's have a go," he smiled.

I was excited to play with the world's best drummer again, maybe too excited. We groped for a groove but barely made a scratch. I put the blame on me, "I'm a bit off. Let's have a go tomorrow."

As soon as Bedford left, I fell into a lonesome funk, but that's okay. Elvis was lonely too.

13 October

Mystery Girl's *Dial M for Mystery* has knocked *Cluster Pain* off its number one peg, but this comes as no surprise. She was bound to go massive with her final release. To quote her interview in NME, "Had always intended to quit while I was ahead. That's why I wore a mask—so I could return to normal life and not be bothered. Now that I've sung my songs, it's time to live my life." Her retirement means less competition for The Blow Goes, so good on us.

A lyric for Cluster Pain:
Meant to watch the news today
But the blues got in my way
I tossed that thing around
Tossed it in the lost and found
'Til the last go round
Of the lost and found
I'm bellerin' plain
From a cluster pain

Jelly vid phoned, sounding knackered, "You must be dead chuffed, writing a number one song." I was freaked seeing how Skeletor she looked with lank hair, glazed eyes, spotty face, and a frame skinnier than Shadrack on a fast.

Jelly asked for a loan to pay her energy bill. Not knowing what she might actually spend it on, said I'd send half. I brought up the drugs.

"Off that stuff now. Know you don't believe me, but I don't care." Jelly's defensiveness gave her away. Minds occupied by foreign powers don't surrender without a fight. As Jelly rapped about her busted life, my thoughts drifted away.

"The illegals started out quite fun," Jelly whined, "How could I judge Johnny if I hadn't tried his poison? So, I tried it once for science, twice 'cause I liked it, and thrice 'cause it was nice. Now the good's gone and so is Johnny, but I need the drugs like air."

Jelly's burned through a score of years in a summer. Just twenty-six, but she could pass for forty.

19 October

Day started when my phone chirped with a pre-arranged interview I'd forgotten, "So Mr. Fumbo, what influences inspired your writing style?" asked Miss Ida Perigreen of *OK Go* magazine.

"Well you see, Miss Perigreen, I conjure a bastard offspring of Bowie's Diamond Dog and Lennon's Walrus slapped upside melodies played on Mellotron strings with added rain stick effects."

"What's it like to go from mental health patient to topping the charts in less than a year?" She asked.

"It's alright ma. I'm only bleeding."

"Did the pressure of recording your album contribute to Bedford Vann's stress?"

"There's a heavy pressure on, but not to worry, Bedford's strong as English oak."

"Is it a thematic album you're planning?"

"Wouldn't say that yet. Not with just a few tracks done and starts on others. Gearly and I plan to press on and finish it the best we can. Beddy will help with final mixes." If I were a praying man, this would be my prayer.

20 October

Last night I finally saw, up close and personal, that man among men, that inestimable professor d'amour, Mister Stu Bilat, height-abbreviated love swami supreme. Jane and I caught his act at the Cheeta Club.

Afterwards. Jane seemed uncharacteristically nervous as we slid into a cushy red leather booth at the hotel bar. I ordered a Margarita. She called for Absinthe with champagne, a heavy drink for her.

Jane took a long gulp of pale green nectar and looked me straight in the eyes, "Something I gotta tell you, baby." she said, quoting a favorite Joe Meek song. "Something's giving me hell now, baby."

I smiled at the reference, expecting she'd follow it with something like, "I'd like to suggest a new look for the band." But she had something quite different in store.

"I'm sorry, know this will shock you, but I don't know how to cushion it. Believe me, I've tried to think of a way. If you feel unfairly deceived — you have every right." She paused, piling up the drama. "The fact is, Fumbo, I've got a rather big secret. It's not fair to keep it from you a second longer. But I have to ask you to swear you'll never tell anyone, no matter what happens. Not anyone, ever. Okay?"

"I'm a spy. I keep secrets." I was so keen to hear her out, I'd have promised anything.

Jane took a deep breath. "Fumbo . . . I . . . I am . . . I am Mystery Girl. Or at least I *was* Mystery Girl."

"What? How do you mean that?"

I studied Jane to see if she was putting me on, but there was no mistaking her serious expression. My world had cleaved in two. On one side was reality as I knew it; on the other was this crazy new bizarro world. Looking closely, there was no mistaking the resemblance. Her eyes and mouth matched. Bodies? Identical. I said, "Don't kid a kidder," but I knew she wasn't. Still, this demanded final confirmation. Jane was ready. After looking about to see if anyone was watching, she reached into her purse, pulled out a micro-thin satin mask and deftly slipped it over her head. I recognized it straight away from her Bad Boy video. She ripped it off and stuffed it in her purse, explaining, "I brought it along in case you didn't believe me."

"But . . . why?"

"Sorry I had to deceive you. You don't deserve that, but I had to stay mum until I saw where things were going with us. Once we developed feelings for each other, it wasn't fair to keep you in the dark. Don't blame you if you want to be rid of me now."

"Rid of you? Don't talk crazy. Funny thing is, I've had a crush on Mystery Girl since the first time I heard her sing. And now I'm dating her? It's a lot to swallow."

"I'm terribly sorry about all this . . ."

"Why did you drop out and kill your career?"

"I was never comfortable with the pop star life, knew that going in. That's why I invented Mystery Girl, so I could hide in plain sight of millions. My plan all along was to check out as soon as I'd fulfilled my musical ambitions and banked sufficient creds."

"If you have major creds banked; why work wardrobe?"

"Fashion's always been a passion. I designed all the Mystery Girl outfits. And, I like working in a team. Just might be a bit addicted to the road, as well. Working wardrobe lets me enjoy the parts of this biz I like, while it takes away the spotlight."

I'm dating Mystery Girl? This is a world within a world. I could taste the multi-verse in my teeth.

21 October

I tossed and turned all night, thinking on Jane's revelation. But why should I care? She's still the same girl I fell in love with. As long as I keep her secret, there shouldn't be any impact on us. But still, *I am dating Mystery Girl*. Mind's officially blown.

Beddy's problems strike a hard blow at the band's future. No tripod can stand on two legs. Up in here, I am depressed. Might be a selfish git, thinking about the band in the midst of Bedford's problems, but he's

happiest when playing music and showing the world
what we've got might prove his best therapy of all

22 October
Dressed and stressed, I gulped a cappuccino and
visited Beddy. "English oak," I said and Beddy smiled.
Looks like the man is back.

Back in my room and feeling happy as Larry, I
plugged in and struck the power chords of The Bliss
Dogs' anthem, *We Believe That We Can't Go Wrong*.

Major Boyle rang. Said he needs to visit Hollywood
for Blow Goes business and wants me along. We're
leaving tomorrow. Having never visited America, I'm
revved up. Beddy will stay behind to rest and Gearly
will hang with him to mix our completed tracks.

I rang Jane with the news. She's coming too.

23 October
Major Boyle, Jane and I are traveling in style on The
Spirit of London, floating across the Atlantic in the
world's coolest dirigible.

Got a text from Bedford, *Let's get busy and finish
the album*.

I stand ready to rock. Gotta new lyric, I replied
attaching this:
Floating down a river
Of plasticine goo
In a glass bottom boat
With a captain in blue
An Earl's Court squid
Appears on the shore
You'd throw him a quid
But he's rather a bore
An annoying little git
Who bothers you in rhyme
You'd like to discuss it
But haven't the time

"That's urgent," Beddy texted and the world seemed
right.

I stared out a porthole at the choppy green Atlantic
below, thinking on New Music Express and their review
of our Gone With The Show EP, *Bedford Vann's*

compositions mark him as a massive talent who deserves a seat amongst the greats. Who can argue with that? But then the wankers added: *"Fumbo's songs, on the other hand, place him firmly in the front row of the second rate.* Just you wait, NME. Just you wait.

29 October
Awoke to America's great southwest desert blazing below in bright sunlight. We ordered fresh-squeezed orange juice, rye toast, scrambled eggs, and cappuccinos. A giant golden eagle soared past our porthole clutching a moody rabbit in its beak. Jane screamed. I reached for my phone's cam, but missed it. Then we got busy in our Viewport Sleeperette as the world floated beneath us.

Scheduled to land at LAX soon, but Jane and I wouldn't have minded the trip continuing a while.

30 October / *Los Angeles, Republic of California*
They push their name "Republic of California" hard. No surprise, given how well the state has prospered since America broke up with itself.

I'm up on the eleventh floor, watching the cruisers below from our room at The New Standard on Sunset Boulevard. Cold rain taps a Bo Diddley rhythm on huge plate glass windows while random blasts of wind flex the panes in and out like they're breathing.

Major Boyle scheduled a recording session at the Capitol tower after I mentioned there's an ancient echo chamber there I'm desperate to try. It sounds positively three-dimensional on Brian Wilson's original *Smile Sessions*.

The sky cleared up so I copped a Hollywood van tour that took me by the newly rebuilt Brown Derby restaurant. Our driver explained, "There's a city-wide programme to bring back the novelty architecture that was popular here in the early twentieth century. They've rebuilt the Bulldog Cafe, the Brown Derby, the Hoot Owl, and Tail o' the Pup, with more soon to follow."

I saw Hollywood Boulevard, the Sunset Strip, The Whiskey-A-Go-Go, Formosa Café, The Mega Corp. Chinese Theater, The Hollywood Bowl, Frolic Room,

Pantages Theater, Hollywood High, and the Griffith Park Observatory. We got out at the Chinese Theater to try matching our footprints with ancient Hollywood greats.

The sky darkened as we pulled up to the hotel. A gentle drizzle soon pounded down with biblical fury.

I tried noodling on keytar, but couldn't concentrate with the storm lashing the windows, so I watched a Twilight Zone episode about a spaceship that crashed on a planet just like modern America, but with everything frozen as stiff as statuary.

An E-Vite came through for a release party, The Hurtin' Kind request your presence at the Whiskey A Go-Go for tonight's show.

Jane texted, Looked up some old friends, love. Off to their house in the Miracle Mile. Back late. Let me know if you go out?

I took a nap, woke up groggy, popped a double espresso from the minibar machine and missed my girl.

I taxied to the Whiskey where I sipped excellent tequila watching The Hurtin' Kind. They were on it, but I was more into second-billed Lazy Susan, a doe-eyed soul slinger backed by twin sisters on keys and drums. She yodeled like an Alpine fraulein, strummed an electric oud, and cooed a koo-koo blues from her album, Straight Outta The Casbah—and that was just the first song. For the second, she beat a talking drum while yelping of love unrequited in polyrhythmic syncopations expressing mixed feelings with artificial string backing.

I worked my way backstage in order to compliment the evening star.

"Fumbo? Of The Blow Goes? I'm charmed." Susan extended a hand. We shook.

"Likewise."

"Gotta minute?" She smiled.

"Now?" I had no idea what she was on about.

"Now is always best." Her smile was contagious.

We piled into her tiny Blunt Force micro and motored to a Hollywood bungalow where I sat in a cosy orange armchair. She whispered, "Pardon me a sec while I get comfy."

Susan undid her top's buttons with the flair of a professional. I snuck stares at her lovely breasts while she switched on a slim wooden box and waved elegant fingers about, coaxing eerie Theremin swoons from her album *Sounds in Space*. She looked gorgeous, her skin burnished golden by candlelight. As she finished the song and smiled, I clapped approval.

Susan ambled to the kitchenette where she filled an electric pitcher. We sat at her kitchen table. An intoxicandle wafted heady fumes as we sipped tea. By the time I had my last sip, I'd slipped into a dreamlike state that ended when Susan kissed me full on the lips, stirring me up man-size. But thoughts curved back to Jane and cooled my ardor. I mumbled something about getting up early and beat a hasty retreat.

Jane was still out with her chums, so I stopped at the hotel bar. A bleak old geezer sat there boring the barkeep's ear off, so I ambled down Sunset Boulevard and popped into a shop where I bought a candle shaped like a Malibu surfer's wave that I gave to Jane later. It proved to be a gateway to a sweet night of love. Jane and I coasted to sleep in a room that smelled like the ocean if it was made of wax and set on fire.

31 October
Beddy texted this morning sounding like his old self. *Getting on well with a girl I met in rehab. We're off to holiday at her family's sheep farm in Scotland. Know it'll happen with the band. I just need a break. Tell Gearly to hang on.*

At least he sounds happy.

I just hope that hundred-foot wave racing towards us flattens out before it hits the beach.

Major Boyle booked me five hours at Capitol's recording studio with a band of Hollywood studio pros and a crack producer. We bungled around getting started, but eventually caught a groove and created a creamy melody for *Plasticine Goo* I'm crazy about. The producer crafted a pop chamber piece complete with backwards guitar, cello, melodic bass, spy guitar, and bongos. With help from him and the players, I'd laid down something good on my first solo session.

1 November

Taxied to Santa Monica Boulevard to visit actors buried in their final plots. An ancient graveyard for show business royalty, Hollywood Forever dominates a seedy stretch where hand-lettered signs promise every empty thrill known to man. Meandered about 'til I came upon a life-sized bronze of Johnny Ramone with rain-etched tear tracks down his metal cheeks. A crudely lettered sign around his neck said: *Gabba-gabba hey*.

I strolled to a placid pond clotted with white swans while my mood ring swirled a funky whirlpool as I thought on all that's gone down with the band's approach to star status. NME even said we are. But without Beddy aboard, I'm like a doomed captain barking commands while his ship burns down around his ankles.

Took a cab back to the hotel where I read Mark Twain's "Adventures of Huckleberry Finn" on MemBrain—the part where Huck and Jim entertain visitors on the raft. Reading it spun my mood ring bright. Three shots of tequila helped, too.

2 November / *Hollywood, California*

Major Boyle flew Gearly over to cut some tracks. I played them the *Plasticine Goo* jam with session players. Boyle liked it and said he'd book time for Gearly and I to finish it up, suggesting we find a replacement drummer to fulfill our touring contract. He's generally pushing us to get on with things sans Beddy. We've mixed feelings about that, but find it hard to make our case.

Auditioning drummers at New Gold Star, we set the would-bes loose on classics: *In a Soylent Way, Crimson And Clever, Tinctures of Billy, The Man Who Snapped Misery's Balance*, and *Screwy Screwy*. It all went smoothly enough, but Gearly and I couldn't swing with their predictably professional percussion. It just made us miss Beddy all the more. Got the studio blues.

Knackered after our session, I returned to the hotel, took a hot bath and sipped a steaming cup of ginger tea. Jelly rang up, sounding out-of-it again. Does anybody remember laughter?

I smoked a spliff from the minibar as I sat on the terrace enjoying a sexy California night while fake ocean scents wafted from my wave candle.

A holo-ad drifted by, *You can fight sleep but you can't fight the sheep. Dream the night away with Naptabs.* I gazed out at charming neon signs glowing through a sudden coastal fog caressing the city of angels to quiet.

3 November
Happiness was born a twin.
~ Lord Byron

Jane and I motored up the Pacific Coast Highway to an Italian bistro in Malibu where we enjoyed Scungilli, Napa wine, and mint-chocolate cake. Afterwards, we sat on a terrace sipping grappa under a full moon.

Looking at me over her wine glass, Jane smiled and said, "Welcome to the Riviera." Often compared to Italy, California showed us why tonight.

As we finished our meal, a light breeze blew through the honey-blonde hair of a beautiful Latina singing Lennon's *Imagine* in a sweetly accented voice accompanied by twin mariachi guitars.

We removed our shoes and trod creaky wooden steps down to the beach. Jane tripped me and we tumbled on the sand, laughing as the ocean laughed back.

We motored to the hotel in a rental Ford Electron accompanied by *Johnny Zhivago's Greatest Hurts*. Tapping this out on MemBrain while Jane enjoys a late night spa visit.

Seems like America's most intense pioneers didn't quit moving until they were forced to stop by the ocean. Their descendants linger in California still. While most of America's newly created countries stagger through poisoned landscapes with cracked economies, California's made the future its bitch.

Had a phone chat with Gearly. We agreed to press on regardless and finish the album with or without our missing-in-action drummer. Studio time is booked, starting tomorrow. If Bedford re-enters the picture so much the better, but we've got to keep moving forward.

4 November

A hotel café breakfast with Jane got the day off to a pleasant start.

I joined Gearly at the studio in the afternoon. We polished up *Plasticine Goo*, an historic occasion, our first recording sans Bedford. The session drummer was tight, but we missed our rhythm king massively.

After work, Jane and I enjoyed spicy Indian food in a private booth draped with paisley sheets at 'Lectric Lasa. The roof rolled back for a sky view as a cool cat named Ravi flipped our wigs with electric sitar jams.

5 November

Breakfast with Gearly at a Hollywood sidewalk café. Geezers are funny here. They look hard to see if you're somebody they wish they knew, then when they figure out you're not, pretend they're too cool to care.

He's rolling with the instrumental bits and I've got lyrics to burn, but they're only words, and words are all I have. Gearly can play any instrument he picks up, and we've got a fat budget for session players—thanks to Boyle, it's sorted. Unfortunately, all the sorting in the world doesn't fill the black hole of Beddy's absence.

Major Boyle hired a Hollywood studio to animate a vid for *Plasticine Goo*. Their storyboard of animated 3D flowers swooning beside a gently moving river while sexy sirens cavort on the shore and neon squids leap skywards to launch double rainbows that morph into the towering figure of a jabbering git who walks down a staircase to the sea pleased us mightily.

Gearly and I had a blast in the studio and that was a huge relief after recent anxieties. Excited about getting on with things, we jammed a bit and wrote *He Casts a Long Shadow*, a medium tempo number about our drummer. Gearly double-tracked zither over a Swiss goat herder's field holler. He blended that with a salty sea chantey and sounds of an armored car blown-up by a rocket-propelled grenade. We cross-faded that with a reverbed banjo plucked on the deck of a Mississippi riverboat as a gospel choir wailed from a clapboard chapel on the shore. I added keytar bass and sang background on a mic with Gearly. "A sure number one," Major Boyle exclaimed, hearing the playback.

Don't mind if we do.

6 November

Jelly rang this morning, "Hello, would this be my darlin' Fumbo?"

"Would this be long lost Jelly?"

"None other. Which side's up?"

"Doing the best I can, considering."

"Considering what?"

"Our drummer's gone missing."

"Sorry. What can you do without a drummer?"

"We'll have to press on regardless."

"Got an extra ticket for three weeks from tonight, a little band you might know, the Black Mantas?" It was good hearing her excited about something besides drugs.

"Isn't this where I came in?" A year had flown by since we last saw the Mantas.

Huh?" Jelly missed my reference.

"Thanks, but I'm spending what little free time I have left with my girl lately."

"Who cares? Meet you at Marble Cross Station exactly three weeks from today, eight sharp. Good enough?"

"Appreciate the offer. But sorry, can't."

"It's more than seeing the show. We need to chat." Jelly purred her patented man-melting voice.

I apologized again, hung up and brewed a cuppa while thinking that maybe I should just hand this diary over to the publisher. They might publish it to capitalize on the heat our band's throwing off. *Troubled Blow Goes' keytarist spills the beans on a year of living dangerously*, or something like that.

A novel in the form of a diary might be a novelty indeed.

10 November

The more I think about it, publishing this diary as a novel would be a neat trick. I re-drafted it for five hours straight before collapsing on a beanbag chair so forcefully that a seam popped, shooting out white

Styrofoam pellets that fell to the carpet, spelling out: *THE END*.

11 November – 5 December / Levanto, Italy

Jane and I enjoyed a lovely train ride to Levanto, Italy. Not quite sure why we decided on a foggy winter holiday on the Mediterranean, but it's quiet out of season and should prove free of distractions so I can concentrate on turning this diary into a book.

Beddy texted from Scotland, "I've fashioned some new tunes. Got demos."

We emailed tracks back and forth with each of us adding bits 'til we were satisfied. I sent them on to Gearly. He added, subtracted, and tweaked until things were ticking like a fine Swiss watch. Boyle was dead chuffed when I emailed him the mixes.

We are tight.

We are The Blow Goes.

And we mean it, man.

7-18 December / South of France

Bedford came 'round to join our sessions at a French chateau where Bowie, T-Rex, and Elton John had laid down classic tracks. We layered parts onto existing starts and recorded new jams hard and soft. The rhythm king is back pounding that kit like only he can, pushing us to finish the album. We voted on a title: *Somewhere Over the Slagheap*.

Considering how well Boyle's propaganda has worked so far, Slagheap could go titanium.

23 December

Jane and I blazed cannabis, sipped champagne and copped a giggle fit tracking Blow Goes' downloads on MemBrain. Who knew we were so big in Croatia? This little band looks unstoppable. Got so happy we decided to create a little Jimmy or Jane to join us.

Boyle has loaded our schedule with promo appearances, interviews, photo sessions, and gigs, allowing little time for you, Dear Diary.

Here's a condensed update:

Our first gig touring Slagheap went down a storm at Hollywood's Greek Theater, an historic outdoor venue where many of our idols have graced the stage. Band morale peaked, aided in no small measure by Mr. Sparky Fuego serving in dual roles as roadie and pal.

Jane and I are nesting at a Malibu beach pad built on a bluff above the sea where the beach blew out due to permanent high tides. It's cool. Our pool has a view of the ocean and, even better; our ocean has a view of the pool.

Tricky Dick resides at The Monkey Mansion, a home for wayward monkeys that Boyle has established as our charity. Dick seems happy there, but I miss my chum.

My song *Plasticine Goo* pulls more streams than any Blow Goes song yet and has proven an audience favorite at gigs. Take that, *New Music Express*. Inspired by its success, I jammed a lyric today.

Mechanical Stan
Was born of a plan
For a new kind of man
A manufactured man
With their lineage trends
Other mechanical men
Made perfect friends
For Mechanical Stan
He hit the beach, but Stan couldn't tan
Not Stan the mechanical man
Resting at the shore 'til he rusted
All his circuits cracked and busted
Things corroded 'til Stan exploded
They swept him into a pan
And recycled that mechanical man
Into a reincarnated son of Stan

25 December / London, England
Celebrated a cozy London Christmas with my beloved in a sweet, pine-scented daze. Love her madly, such a magic time.

Tomorrow I turn this diary over to an interested publisher. Major Boyle negotiated a fat contract due to The Blow Goes' buzz. They're publishing it as the book you're reading now. Having this diary in print feels like a serious invasion of privacy, but the healthy advance check soothes my anxieties remarkably.

Feeling so good, I've made an appointment to have my mind chip and embedimeds removed.

31 January 2049 / Havana, Cuba

Beddy and I flew to Cuba for a holiday with the wives. They deserve a treat; they've been in our corner every step of this daft trip.

Plunking an African thumb piano while gazing out to sea, I spied Jane walking the Malecon below. A breeze flipped up her hat brim, exposing my favorite face in the world. She sensed me staring, looked up, smiled, and waved. I waved back. She blew a kiss.

14 February 2049 / New York City

We've returned stateside for a Valentine's Day charity gig to benefit an animal rescue charity setting up the Monkey Mansion. Boyle booked us at Madison Square Garden on a bill with Black Mantas and Native Gold, Deathrow Jethro's band sans leader. Jane suggested surprising the audience by doing a walk on as Mystery Girl at the end of our set to sing *Bad Boy* in full mask and leatherette. I'm wild about her idea. Might just blow the audience a whole new blowhole

28 February 2049

As I stood atop a thirty-foot speaker stack in thigh-high gumboots and Buckingham guard's cut-away coat, I held up a hand to stop the band and stepped up to the microphone, "We have a surprise for you tonight, a certain mysterious missing miss has consented to a re-enter the spotlight in order to support this fine cause. Ladies and gentlemen, may I present our evening star, Mystery Girl?"

Fifty thousand fans roared approval as my wife strode across the stage looking like she's never done one wrong thing.

Fade to black.

GLOSSARY

A
Arse: English term, ass
Ambi-sound: Future brand, a music playback system

B
Barmy: English slang, crazy
Blancmange: English term, a pudding
Bliterade: Future brand, a stimulating soft drink stronger than current day caffeinated beverages
Bollocks: English slang, nonsense
Boyo: Future slang, a boyfriend
Bugger: English slang, various meanings, like bloody it has no American equivalent

C
Calmz: A future brand, anti-anxiety medication
Chuffed: English term, pleased
Codswallop: English slang, something silly or untrue
Convo: Future slang, a conversation
Cred: Future slang, a digital monetary unit
Cuppa: English slang, a cup of tea

D
Devil's tail: Future slang, a powerful illegal stimulant
Disturbo: Future slang, a mentally disturbed person
Dum-dum boy: Future slang, street thug

E

Embedi-med: Future term, a medical prescription embedded in the body
Ener-Tea: Future brand, a stimulating beverage

F
Fringe: English slang, hairstyle with bangs

G
Geezer: English slang, a guy
Git: English slang, a bastard

H
H-Bloc Subsidized: Future term, government subsidized housing
Holo: Future slang, a hologram
Holo-sign: Future term, holographic advertising or signage
Hover: Future slang, a helicopter

I
Illegals: Future slang, black market or illegal drugs
Innerlude: Future brand, a sleep aid
Intoxi-candle: Future term, a candle that produces psychoactive smoke

K
Keytar: Keyboard instrument worn with a strap like a guitar
Kip: English term, a nap
Knackered: English term, tired, exhausted
Knocked down: Future slang, argued

L
Laffro dazzler: Future slang, funny
Lift: English term: an elevator
Loo: English term: a restroom

M
Melon: Future slang: a person's head or brain

Mellotron: an early electronic keyboard instrument that plays pre-recorded tape loops of instruments, usually strings

MemBrain: Future term, a paper thin, foldable computer with a floating holographic screenMind-chip: Future term, an implant that regulates psychology

Minky: Future slang, sexy

N

Nap tab: Future brand, a sleeping pill

Nutri-Bar: Future brand, nutritional candy bar

Nutter: English slang, an insane person

Nicked: English slang, stole

O

Offy: Future slang, one who practices an alternative lifestyle by living off the grid

Omni: Future Term, an implant that serves as, ID, credit card and uplink portal, also called a wrist omni

P

PeepPals: Future brand, a social networking site

Plasticine: English term, modeling clay

Presser: English slang, a press conference

Punter: English slang, a customer

Q

Quay: English term, a pier

Qwik-Charge: Future term, a charging station for electric vehicles

R

Rapido: Present and future brand, a Cuban fast food chain

Repli-bot: Future term, a robot built to replicate an individual human

Robo: Future slang, a robot

S

Sacked: English slang, Fired from a job

Showbubble: Future term, A spherical
entertainment venue
Shinky: Future slang, "Cool" or desirable
Suss: English term, Understand or figure out
Skint: English term, broke, without funds
Slag: English slang, an insult or put down
Sod it: English slang, "Forget about it"
Stimi: Future slang, a highly caffeinated soft drink
Stoppers: English slang, brakes

T
Telly: English slang, television
Tosser: English slang, a masturbator

U
Uni: Future slang, one piece jumpsuit used as
every day clothing

V
Vegeplast: Future term, plastic made from vegetable
matter
Vendi girl: Future term, a feminine-appearing robot
that sells retail items
Vid: Future slang, a video

W
Wanker: English slang, masturbator
Winkle pickers: English slang, shoes with extremely
pointed toes

Wrist Omni: Future Term, implanted chip that serves
as debit card, pharmaceutical dispenser, online portal
and identification

Author's Biography

James Cherry grew up moving around, finally settling in Manhattan, where he worked as an illustrator. Relocating west, he turned to writing, edited websites and wrote for publication. This is his second novel. "Coronado '92" came first.

Author's photo by Mike Cherry

THANKS TO

GEORGE HUFFMAN
DYLAN DRAY
MARK LONDON
MARTIN AMIS
GEORGE ORWELL
ANTHONY BURGESS
KURT VONNEGUT
JACK KEROUAC
MARK TWAIN
JACK LONDON
DAVID BOWIE
RON CARRAHER
BRIAN ENO
RAY BRADBURY
KIM ROBERSON
FRANCINE RULEY
LILI CHIN
EDDIE MORT
and
ALDOUS HUXLEY

James Cherry's first novel is also available.

'A week long trip to the Coronado District in pistol hot early nineties Phoenix, it captures snatches from the lives of a tapestry of colorful characters just trying to get on, an artist, model, poet, dancer and couple make the suburban "God Forsaken Hellhole" in the desert southwest somewhat hip and tolerable, even with a neighborhood killer on the loose. Feels like Hunter S. Thompson in its counter cultural ruminations."
    - Michael Arturo